THE ALPHA'S PET

LOKI RENARD

Published by Stormy Night Publications and Design, LLC.
www.StormyNightPublications.com

Cover design by Korey Mae Johnson
www.koreymaejohnson.com

Images by 123RF/Julia Onuchina, 123RF/Eric Isselee, and
Bigstock/Wisky

1st Print Edition. June 2016

ISBN-13: 978-1534810709

ISBN-10: 1534810706

FOR AUDIENCES 18+ ONLY

CHAPTER ONE

"You will obey me, pet…"

The words were growled in the quivering woman's ear, her naked body arched against the firm grip Alexei had taken of her hair, dark tresses gathered in his fist. She was covered in sweat, which beaded over her heated skin and dripped on the marble floor.

Her will was strong, but his was stronger. Alexei could not see her face, but he could sense her defiance and her desire in equal measure as she writhed beneath him.

He felt more alive than he had in a decade, challenged by this little wench whose flowing lust made it clear she wanted him even as she refused to submit. He let out a growl and fastened his teeth on the back of her neck hard enough for her to feel it as a tight pinch, holding her in place as her red bottom rose and fell beneath his hips, her well spanked cheeks glowing with heat and a hue that made those curves all the more alluring to his rampant hardness.

She had intruded in his territory, defied his will, and even now she was refusing to answer the simplest of questions. He burned to know who she was, or simply to see her face but they seemed locked in their positions, him on top, her beneath.

"Tell me your name," he said, lifting his mouth from her neck as his hardness ran along the folds of her sex, the last bastions of defense against him. They were soft and they were wet, welcoming him as he

1

began to sink inside her and be engulfed in the tightest, hottest little...

"Alexei?"

The dour tones of his majordomo and beta woke Alexei from his dream. He came to consciousness with a snarl directed at Vladimir, who stood next to his bedside, formally dressed in the dawn light and looking as he always did, utterly staid and respectable.

"There had better be a fire," Alexei said, making no effort to hide the tent of his erection that propped up the sheet covering his muscular form.

"You requested to be woken at a reasonable hour," Vladimir reminded him. "You will remember, we have a guest arriving today."

"Of course I remember," Alexei said, throwing back the sheet and striding across the room, magnificent in his nakedness. He spoke over his shoulder as he entered his bathroom. "The little Englishwoman. How could I forget?"

The dream stayed with Alexei long after his shower. He thought of it as he fastened cufflinks on his starched white shirt and briefly glanced at himself in the highly polished antique mirror. He looked as he had always looked: handsome, but hard. His features leant themselves to a stern, perhaps even severe demeanor that persisted though he was actually quite happy in that moment.

It was a historic day. The Russian pack was to receive new blood, the first in several generations. A woman, one who had proved too defiant for the alpha of one of England's oldest packs to manage. Alexei went to his desk and looked at the details of her arrival once more. The alpha Lorcan Wallace had been kind enough to provide detailed information, including a photograph.

Alexei's long, strong finger drifted over the image of the proud woman staring defiantly into the camera as if she could will anyone who so much as beheld her image to cower. She had a beauty that refused to be delicate, but he could sense a certain vulnerability in her, which he had no doubt was fiercely guarded behind the hard exterior that had been captured by the photographer.

"Hello, Sacha," he murmured. It was a cute name, a diminutive moniker in his language, though the woman in the picture did not seem to know it.

From the moment the letter containing the picture had arrived, Alexei's interest had been piqued. He picked the letter up again, though he did not need to read it. He had read it so many times he knew it by heart. It was a request, desperate, but polite, for him to take possession of Sacha, bring her into his pack and give her a home.

Sacha. Strange for an Englishwoman to have such a title. Was it mere chance that she had been given what was so close to a Russian name but for one little c? The act of a creative parent? He doubted it. Alexei had tangled with fate far too many times to be so foolish as to think the world ran rudderless on dumb luck. This one was meant for him, he was certain of it. Her imminent arrival had his blood running hot. It had been many years since a woman had excited him so. Strange, given that he had never met her before. Never even heard her voice. And yet she had invaded his imagination and his dreams.

Perhaps he was growing fanciful at the ripe old age of forty. She was, after all, being expelled from her pack. She was not coming to him because she had any love for Russia or desire to join a new family. She was being cast out and if not for him she would become a lone wolf. Alexei suspected that her brother's desire for him to take charge of her had nothing to do with his concern that she would not be able to function on her own. The look of defiance in her silent gaze told him that she would almost certainly survive as a single woman, if not thrive. He was more likely worried that unless someone else had charge of her, she would come back and perhaps challenge him for his pack.

Alexei had chuckled when the subtext of the letter had become clear. The English alpha was both afraid for, and of, the woman he was sending. Alexei did not share that fear. It was quite clear to him that this little woman with the dark hair and golden eyes had been allowed far too much leeway in her pack of origin, and as a result she had grown to be what her alpha brother described in his British way as 'problematic.' The English were usually true to form in their talent for understatement.

Alexei thoroughly expected a challenge once Sacha Wallace arrived in his domain. It was a challenge he looked forward to with no small measure of anticipation.

CHAPTER TWO

Sacha did not like Russia at first glance. Not on second glance either. In fact, no amount of glances improved her impression of the icy wasteland she found herself standing in. Cold air whipped at her face, stinging her mouth and nose. The temperature was below freezing point and everything that would have been wet instead was transformed to ice. She had not expected the weather to be so inclement. She had not thought of the weather at all as she was being bundled into a, driven to an airstrip, and forcibly deported from the land of her birth.

Sacha had never been one for travel, and did not like being so far from home. Of course, she didn't have a home anymore. Not since her traitorous brother had chosen the life of his little once-human whore and cast her out for daring to challenge the new order.

She had been the only passenger on the chartered plane, which had landed twenty minutes ago and departed just five minutes later. Sacha stood alone on the tarmac at a remote Russian airport, shivering in a coat that was far too thin. She had to hand it to Lorcan; he had made absolutely sure she would not be able to escape or evade her fate. The plane had flown her directly into the heart of another alpha's

5

territory. There had been no opportunity to disembark at any major airport, and there were no planes to catch out of the so-called airport she was at. She was thousands of miles away from anywhere hospitable, left to wait for the arrival of the local alpha's escort.

Far from the imposing figure she had cut back at the manor, Sacha looked small and slender against the vastness of the landscape, her dark figure diminutive against the great white plains of snow and ice spread out all around her. Her luggage was stacked beside her, three great trunks containing all she owned. Lorcan had been generous enough to allow her to take some things from the family home before sending her away, never to return.

Shivering, Sacha looked around yet again for some kind of shelter, knowing already that there was none. The one-roomed 'airport' behind her was closed for the day, or perhaps the year. There were no lights on inside and little in the way of indication that it had been used any time in recent memory. Drifts of snow had built up around the sealed doors, and the only signs were in Cyrillic script, which she could not read. The area around the airstrip seemed uninhabited. It was a large plain, bordered at the very edges of her vision with belts of trees. She saw no sign of human habitation or traffic. Once the plane departed, a deep snowy silence had settled over the earth, leaving her with nothing but the sound of her own thoughts.

In contrast to the cold around her, hot rage burned inside her chest as she realized just how desperate her position truly was. She had been abandoned. She had been maligned. She had been cast out, but she was not broken, nor was she in the least bit sorry for what she'd done. As the cold closed in all the more, her shivering grew intense.

She found it both strange and insulting that she had not been met upon arrival. A woman of her stature should have been greeted by the alpha and his retinue. Perhaps they had gotten the time wrong. Or perhaps they had no intention of coming for her at all. In spite of her pride, Sacha started to feel a little bit afraid as the sun slipped ever further toward the horizon. If night were to fall, or even if she were to remain alone a few minutes more, she would have to shift and take her wolf form. As a wolf she would have a warm coat and the hunting prowess to find food. She did not wish to meet the Russians in what Lorcan would have called her beast mode, however. She wished to make her position and intentions clear from the outset, and to do that she needed her linguistic faculties.

It was with a great sense of relief that she caught motion out of the corner of her eye. Something was moving in the distance. Over a period of minutes, it drew closer and she saw that it was a simple white van. If she had been back home it would have belonged to a plumber or some other laborer. It stood to reason that such simple, lowbrow transportation would be sent for her. These Russians were not impressing her with their timeliness or their sense of style.

Sacha sighed inwardly. This really was not nearly good enough. Back home she had driven only the finest of automobiles and had never suffered any discomfort. Now she found herself standing in the snow like some kind of vagrant waiting for the local television repairmen to pick her up.

In due course, and showing no sign of any kind of urgency, the van drew up beside her and three dark-haired men disembarked. Sacha knew at first glance that none of them were alpha. They were brawny and brutish in appearance, but they were not dominant. The corner of her crimson lip lifted as the first approached her.

"Sacha?" He said her name with a guttural growl.

Low-ranking and dull-witted to boot. Who the hell else would be standing out there?

"Do you get a great many visitors?" She asked the question with her usual haughty demeanor, the tone that would have made her pack start belly crawling. It did not have such a pronounced effect upon the Russians. They did not know her yet. They would soon enough.

He didn't answer her question. Instead he pointed to the van.

"Get in."

Sacha was not accustomed to taking orders, certainly not from low-level pack members like the ones who had been sent to retrieve her. During her flight from England she had imagined that she would be met either by the pack's alpha, or perhaps, if he were paranoid, by a security detail of his best men. After all, she was being exiled for an attempted coup. Surely that warranted a little care in her handling.

What she had not been expecting was to be picked up by three men who looked like they did odd jobs around the house. Not dominant men. Not soldiers. Just... men. She started with haughty disapproval at the one who had given her the utterly untenable order, wondering if any of them would understand her if she were to tell them what absolute cretins they were.

"Put my bags in your vehicle." She returned an order for an order. It was met with another round of blank stares.

"Bags!" She pointed at her luggage. "In van!" She pointed at the van as she spoke loudly and slowly.

She was gratified when the two other men started to do her bidding. The first did not move or say a word. He simply stared at her as if he'd never seen a woman capable of giving an order before. That did not surprise Sacha. Wolf packs tended to be patriarchal. Her brother had attempted to lead their pack that way too, but he had not succeeded where she was concerned, and she did not intend on bowing down to any of these Russian men either.

"Get in." The order was repeated bluntly once her baggage was loaded.

She lifted her top lip in a snarl, her golden eyes narrowing as she contemplated violence. Her mood was deteriorating by the moment and the repeated attempts to order her about were hastening the erosion of her last vestiges of self-control. If any of the members of her pack had spoken to her that way she would have flayed them alive.

The stare-down standoff ended when the leader of the little group snapped another order, this time at his men. Sacha didn't speak Russian, but she figured out the context quickly enough as the two lower-ranked men took hold of her and physically threw her into the van with a distinct lack of ceremony.

She stumbled and had to grab the seats so as not to fall as the van door slid shut behind her with a heavy clank. This was shaping up more like an abduction than a greeting. Her three captors piled into the front of the van, squeezed in shoulder to shoulder.

Stuck in the back with her luggage, Sacha fumed. If she had been at home she would have ripped their throats out, but far from any kind of civilization in the wastes of Russia she had little choice but to accept the indignity as they put the van in gear with a decent amount of clanking and swearing and set off away from the airport.

There was little in the way of landscape with which to distract herself. No rolling hills. No sheep dotting fields. Just snow and ice and the occasional dead tree. It was the most austere and depressing scene she had ever laid eyes on and it made her yearn for home so badly her chest physically ached with the desire to see her native land once more. Sitting in the back of the jolting van, she swore to leave this wasteland, return to England, and take her place as pack alpha. She would banish Lorcan and his little whore bride and let them live in exile instead. Darkwood Manor was her rightful home and she would reclaim it one day. For the moment she assuaged her anxieties with thoughts of revenge as she sat in the van, which reeked of beetroot and onions, soil and sweat.

Every moment she spent in the van made her rage grow. She deserved better than this. She was born for more than this. The men transporting her barely gave her a second glance. That she did not understand. At the manor she had drawn the eye and attention of every man. She was a beautiful woman. She knew that in the same way she knew snow was cold and water was wet, not with any ego, but as a simple fact. Her figure was slim but relatively powerful; she had beautiful golden eyes rimmed with long dark lashes, high cheekbones, a straight nose just prominent enough to give her character. She was not pretty. She was not cute. But she did have a certain cold charisma that made men quiver. Usually.

Things were quite clearly different in Russia.

Sacha kept watch over the course of the journey, deeply interested to see where she was going to end up. She doubted it would be nice. The van did not indicate any kind of wealth or style. She could picture the grim Soviet-style architecture where these men probably lived: concrete walls, narrow windows, no charm or aesthetic sense whatsoever. It was going to be difficult to adjust to austere Russian living. Sacha had lived all her life in the stately home of Darkwood Manor, an impressive, historically significant building nestled in English moorland. She missed it terribly. She missed the scent of the place, she missed the familiarity of it. Most of all she missed the sense she'd always had of being tied to the land. England was her home. Her territory. Russia was not.

As Sacha battled with despair, the van slowed and turned off the main road, such as the bleak stretch of asphalt was. She braced herself for some concrete monstrosity to come looming out of snowy wastes, but as the van trundled up an incline, far from being confronted by some soulless concrete monolith, she saw a mansion that took her breath away. The lower stories of the building were like a French palace, multiple stone stairs leading up a steep incline to the house proper, which was ringed with strong columns and balustrades and great arched windows in which a multitude of lights burned. The upper stories were made of wood, turrets and gables and more columns of wood instead of stone. This was no crumbling bunker. This was a building in which old had been married with new in a way that had Sacha agog. It was an architectural marvel complete with statues lining the drive, wolves in various forms, and men caught between animal and man. The place had presence and life and even at a distance Sacha knew it was completely unlike her family home, which was traditional and quiet and sedate.

The van stopped at the foot of the main stone staircase and she was curtly ordered out. She barely paid any attention to the rudeness; she was far too fascinated by her new surroundings. She was led up more stairs than she could count and in through doors that opened into a grand foyer richly decorated with all manner of carpets and ornaments, great golden urns and old vases, and paintings from the masters of bygone eras. The display of wealth was quite unexpected. Sacha judged it gaudy, but she was also impressed. Every surface was clean and polished. There was a staff here, or more likely, members of the pack who performed the duties of domestics with unmistakable pride. She could see her face in the polished bannisters of the great spiral staircase that dominated the space.

With this much wealth at the alpha's disposal it made even less sense to Sacha that a simple van and three dullards had been sent to get her. She was almost certain that there was a fleet of much more suitable vehicles garaged nearby. But perhaps the choice of van was not insignificant. Messages were being sent. They wanted her to know that she was not important. Given the lack of care that had been shown regarding her arrival she was half surprised she hadn't been dragged in the servant's entrance and summarily imprisoned. But if they had done that, then she would not have seen the pack's riches... this was all a game being played with her. She was sure of it. It did not please her.

She may have been arriving in disgrace, but she refused to be shamed and she refused to be cowed by their less than respectful welcome. The van driver left her standing in the foyer with nothing but another one of his irritating orders.

"Wait."

Sacha stood on an ornate rug and waited. And fumed. And plotted. Several people came up and down the stairs while she was standing there. Most of them ignored her. A few cast curious glances. The younger ones, mostly. It was with a cramp of jealousy that Sacha realized this was a thriving pack. This was a great extended family happily reproducing. Mothers rearing young. Youths taking their place in the hierarchy.

She had been under their roof for mere seconds and yet scent and sound told her everything she needed to know. This was how Darkwood Manor should have been. This was the kind of pack she had always dreamed of creating— would have created, if only Lorcan had allowed her to turn new blood. Now she stood in the very heart of her deepest desires, a stranger to everyone, an outcast barely accorded any courtesy at all. Lorcan could not have picked a more perfect punishment if he had tried.

Deep in her miserable thoughts, Sacha did not notice that she was about to be greeted.

"Ms. Sacha Wallace."

Her name rolled off the tongue of a tall man with great soulful dark eyes and raven hair slicked back with an abundance of product in a style that was utterly anachronistic. He came down the spiral staircase slowly, moving with elegance and grace, those eyes making a complete inspection of her disgruntled form. Sacha observed him just as he observed her. He was in his early thirties with a grim demeanor that spoke to power. This must be the alpha. He was certainly dressed like one. His suit was impeccable. As he drew closer, Sacha recognized the fineness of the stitching and the tailoring of the jacket especially. In spite of all these things he was not as impressive as she had expected. The mansion had given an illusion of grandeur that was not quite lived up to in the man who was a little too polished and perhaps even pretty to be truly imposing. That fact made Sacha feel a little better.

"I am Sacha," she said, looking him up and down. "You are the alpha of this pack?"

The man emitted a little snort as if the notion of him being alpha were quite silly. "I am Vladimir Petrosian. I am the majordomo of this household. I administer domestic affairs and have charge of certain members, you among them. Come."

Another curt order. Sacha truly was tired of them, but she was equally tired of standing in the foyer alone. Surely this man would lead her to a room in which she could relax. She was interested in seeing what her accommodations would be like. At home she had most of a wing to herself, but at home the house had been largely empty. She did not expect as much space here, but it looked as though luxury would be ample in various other ways.

Vladimir led her up the grand spiral staircase, ascending three floors to the very top of the building, which was comprised of turrets and altered attics. The main floors were well lit and carpeted with the finest wool rugs and decorated with all manner of paintings. The very top floor was not nearly as fine. It was comfortable, certainly, but there was little in the way of adornment and the fittings and furnishings were much cheaper. Functional rather than fashionable. It almost felt as though they had stepped backstage, away from the fine performance of the rest of the mansion, to the place where the simple people toiled to make the rest of the place look so good. It was clear to Sacha that this was where lower-ranked pack members lived. It seemed her humiliation was not yet complete. Exile was not enough. These Russians clearly intended to make her aware of her new lack of status in every way.

The majordomo led her down the main hall and stopped at a door that subsequently opened into a long room with six beds in it. The room was perhaps twelve feet wide, lit by three small windows that looked out into the snowy wastes. The beds were small and narrow, iron framed, and covered with simple linens that Sacha could see even at a distance were far too thin.

There were a couple of women in the room already, young women in their early twenties perhaps. Upon seeing Vladimir they let out little squeals and escaped through the rear door.

"Interesting effect you have on people," Sacha mused aloud.

"If I am seen up here, it is usually with a cane in my hand," Vladimir explained flatly. "Those two are due elsewhere. They are scheduled to work in the kitchens, so I believe. I expect my presence has served as a reminder."

"So your own pack runs from you," Sacha replied. "Hardly the level of discipline I would have expected."

He raised a brow in her direction. "You will become well acquainted with the level of discipline here very soon."

Sacha returned his gaze without blinking. She was not some scared young woman to squeal and run.

"Why are we in this room?"

"This will be your room."

"No, it won't," Sacha replied flatly. "I do not share my sleeping space."

"Single rooms are reserved for ranking members," Vladimir informed her. "You are an exile. As such you will…"

"No," Sacha interrupted him. "I will not share quarters. I will not be ordered about. Where is the alpha? I wish to see him."

"He does not meet whelps."

Whelp. He'd called her a whelp. Sacha's pride was stung, but she appreciated the irony. She had called Lorcan's bride a whelp on first meeting too, and look where she was now. Ruling the pack. That scrappy little human had not paid Sacha any mind, and Sacha was not going to roll over for this man either.

"Take me to the alpha. Immediately." She fixed the majordomo with a steely glare.

Her look was returned with interest. Vladimir seemed

insulted that she was not accepting her lot as one of a half-dozen single bitches kept in a dormitory awaiting the use of the pack as some kind of servant.

"I am a ranking member of my pack…"

"You have no pack," Vladimir corrected her. "You are an exile. Alexei agreed to take you in so you were not alone. You will earn your place in this pack. And you will start in this room."

"Who is Alexei?"

"Alexei Chernov. Alpha. You know nothing about this pack, do you." He spoke with grave judgment and disappointment, as if he had expected better from her.

"I didn't have a chance to study while I was being cast out," she replied, her tone dripping with derision. "There was a distinct lack of guides to this pack on the plane, and it's not as if anybody has taken the time to speak with me in anything remotely resembling a friendly or informative fashion. I have been treated with all the courtesy accorded to a turnip."

Her lecture only served to make Vladimir's dour expression even dourer. His lips had thinned to an almost imperceptible line and his brows had risen nearly to his hairline. He was little other than two narrowed eyes and flared nostrils by that point.

"You speak out of turn," he said. "I expect to hear three words from you from this point on, in the following combinations. Yes, sir or no, sir."

Sacha snorted. "That might work with your little girls here, Vlad, but I am not so easily broken. Take me to your alpha so that we might come to some more suitable arrangement. You are wasting your time with me."

"On that, we can agree," Vladimir said, his lip curling in disdain. He clearly did not like her very much and the feeling was mutual. If he could have whipped her on the spot, he likely would have, but he was probably only capable of disciplining giggling young women who didn't dare challenge him.

"Take me to Alexei," she ordered. "Now."

Vladimir took in a deep slow breath, then nodded, his eyes hooded as if he knew something she did not. "Very well," he said. "I think you will regret seeing him before you have had a chance to settle and accept your place, but clearly you do not appreciate mercy when you are shown it."

"I do not need mercy," Sacha replied proudly.

"And you shall likely not receive it," Vladimir replied coolly.

Sacha allowed herself a dark little smirk as he turned and led her from the bedroom. This majordomo did not have the slightest idea who he was dealing with. He thought he could raise a brow and flare a nostril and have her yelp and run like the little whelps tarrying in their bedroom. He was just beginning to learn how very wrong he was.

CHAPTER THREE

The alpha's office was as large and spacious as the dining room at Darkwood Manor. There was a large stone fireplace in which a fire was burning, and around it were chairs and couches upholstered in the finest fabrics and made of exotic woods. At one side of the room there were bookcases and shelves containing curiosities and various treasures, a desk that contained papers and pens, but no sign of any electronic technology. On the far side of the room, great windows looked out over the icy plains, frosted at their edges by winter's touch. It was the perfect spot from which an alpha could survey his domain.

It was large enough that there were columns supporting the roof in several places, ornately carved into what looked to Sacha to be stories. There were wolves and there were men all contorted in various dramatic positions. Much like the rest of the room, there was a symbolic weight to the images and even though she did not know the stories they referred to, she felt a reaction forming in her body in response to the art.

"Hello, my dear." A thickly accented voice greeted her from behind, gravelly yet smooth tones dripping with refinement. "Welcome to Voindom—the house of my ancestors and your new home."

"Those are the first words of welcome I have received since I stepped off the plane," Sacha snapped angrily. His arrival had taken her by surprise, and that embarrassed her. She turned to face the speaker and the words died on her lips.

Alexei was stunning. Laying eyes on him made her feel as though she had been punched in the gut. All the air went out of her and she was left staring wordlessly at the man who looked as though he had stepped out of the pages of an alternative high-end fashion magazine. He had a long face hewn by the gods into hard planes and angular lines, strong and naturally harsh in aspect. He was dark-haired with a thick streak of gray extending back from the left temple. His eyes were a stormy dark blue beneath thick but angular brows, giving him a perpetually questioning gaze that pierced the very heart of anyone receiving it.

Sacha stared daggers at him, feeling hostility and fear rising in her, one related to the other. He was tall, much taller than her and his body was muscular in a sinewy sort of way. He was lean and he was almost certainly mean. She saw it in the set of his mouth, the way his upper lip curled when he looked at her. Ruthlessness emanated from him, and though his words were welcoming, she could feel the cold steel beneath them.

So this was what it was like to meet a true alpha. Lorcan, her brother was also alpha, but she had never seen him in that light. They had grown up as siblings. She had seen him skin his knee and lose his teeth. When she looked at him she still saw the gawky boy he'd once been.

She could not imagine Alexei as ever having been young. He was much older and much, much more powerful than her. She could smell his potency even at a distance. Sacha was thoroughly intimidated, but she had no intention of letting her fear show.

"You certainly took your time," she said, forcing brave words over a reluctant tongue. Her voice quivered a fraction toward the end of the sentence.

Alexei's brow rose a fraction of a hair. It was enough to make her feel sick with nerves.

"You come from a small, rural pack," he said with what she sensed was deceptive casualness. "There you were, as the English say, a big fish in a small pond. This is a much larger pond, and you are a much smaller fish than you imagine. Listen to Vladimir and to the other girls. They will be invaluable guides in making your life here."

The 'other girls' were hardly suitable companions. Sacha was no girl. She was a fully grown woman, older than the others by several years.

"I hardly think that a room full of whelps is suitable company for a woman of my station," she informed him. "I am not some stray grateful for straw to sleep on and the scraps from the table to feed on. For generations my bloodline has ruled the south west of England, and I expect the respect that is due me."

Her voice started to crack as her mouth got dry. Talking to Alexei that way was hard work; she felt as though she were pushing through some invisible barrier just to get the words out. His glare had the capacity to make her want to curl up and whimper, but she couldn't give into that impulse. She kept her head high, her eyes locked on his, her spine straight and her shoulders back, her bearing proud as she stood her ground and made her demands.

· · · · · · ·

She was arrogant, the little Englishwoman. And she was completely out of place and out of luck. Alexei had no patience for insubordination in his pack. It was a pity that he would have to be harsh with her. True shifters, born shifters, they were becoming increasingly rare. Laying eyes on Sacha was a true pleasure. She was much more beautiful than her picture had suggested. Her dark hair framed a face of utterly captivating features. Her nose was long and straight, her cheekbones were high, her lips were thinned with the effort of anger, but even so she had a unique beauty, her pale skin and strong features suiting her haughty demeanor perfectly. She almost seemed immune to her situation, but her eyes betrayed the set of her lips and the cocky lift of her chin. They were golden yellow and filled with more emotion than she should be able to contain. Anger. Fear. Pride. Desire. All were locked in that silent gaze that drew him in and did not let him go.

He was quite stunned, truth be told. His pack was full of appealing women, but none of them were like this one. There was no doubt about it. The English alpha had made him a valuable gift. Sacha was a precious jewel, beautiful and proud. He was exceedingly pleased with her, but it would do her no good to know that.

"You are right," he said, watching her eyes brighten for a moment. "A room full of whelps is not a suitable place for you. You are less than a whelp. Our pups are better behaved than you. You should be put in the nursery, where you might learn some manners."

She bristled before him, but in addition to the rage gleaming in her eye, he also saw the blush that ran to the very roots of her hair. His words had excited her. It was often that way. Females who thought themselves dominant were more entranced by submission than even the lowest ranking omega. She did not know it yet, but she would soon beg for both his lash and his domination.

As he watched her react to his words with a silent cacophony of physical responses, Alexei felt a spark of excitement that he had not experienced in a very long time. There was a particular pleasure to be found in taking a proud woman and making her see what she really was deep inside. The one standing in front of him reminded Alexei of another young woman, one he had lost many years ago. She now slept in the icebound ground outside the mausoleum. Outside it because she never did like to be caged or contained, and because that had been the very last thing he

20

could do for her.

For a brief moment, Katya's face swam before his eyes. She had looked nothing like the woman standing before him, and yet, for a second, he saw her in Sacha's eyes. Katya had never been one for obedience either.

With some effort, Alexei forced himself to focus on the matter and the woman at hand. Sacha was not Katya. She was a stranger in what must seem to her to be a very strange land. She was looking to establish herself. Now he thought about it, putting her with the single women was probably a bad idea. She would do her best to dominate them, and either she would fail—probably in bloody fashion—or she would succeed and be on her way to climbing the ranks. That he did not want. She could not be allowed to unsettle the pack, and he did not want to see any of his charges harmed.

"I will not put you with the other single women," he said. "You would be nothing but a bad influence."

She smiled a dark smile, white teeth and canines flashing at him. "You may count on that," she agreed. "You will soon see what this pup is capable of."

Though she was much smaller than him in both stature and bulk, Sacha did an admirable job of staring him down. Through her bravado he could scent her fear. She was doing such a good job of hiding it that it would have been missed by anyone who did not have the senses of a shifter. Unfortunately for the newest, most reluctant member of his pack, both Alexei and Vladimir had excellent senses. For all she postured and spoke in those cultured English tones, her scent meant that she may as well have been cowering with her tail between her legs. A frightened wolf could be dangerous, and this one had already proved herself to be too much for one pack. Alexei knew he would have to handle her with care.

He exchanged a glance with Vladimir. His second in command looked at him with a raised brow, thoroughly unimpressed with her. Alexei knew Vladimir well enough to know that he was probably already mentally picking out the cane he intended on using on her. Vladimir was known as the house disciplinarian. Truth be told, he enjoyed the task. There was perhaps a drop of the sadist in his character, though he was scrupulously fair and never gave a punishment that wasn't deserved. Unfortunately for Sacha, she already deserved some kind of discipline. Her tone was utterly unacceptable, and her attitude would not be tolerated.

$$\bullet \bullet \bullet \bullet \bullet \bullet \bullet$$

Standing between the two men, Sacha tried her best not to be frightened. Either one of them would have been intimidating alone. Together, they not only had her outnumbered, but the imbalance of power was palpable. It was not going to be as easy to assert herself as she had imagined. Her bold words were lacking bite, and that would not do.

The alpha's eyes were still locked on her. They had not left her since she'd turned to face him. He had the gaze of a dominant animal. Sacha had used the same technique on her own pack members—maintain eye contact until they began to squirm and were forced to break it. She had not been on the receiving end of it to this extent before. It was quite a novel experience, to feel as though she was shrinking before Alexei, becoming smaller and smaller by the second.

She could feel Vladimir behind her too, his dour energy matching Alexei's in intensity. She did not know how a man could be so reserved and yet so intimidating.

"Be careful with your words, pup," Alexei drawled. "And be even more careful with your actions. We believe in consequences here. This is not a permissive pack, as you will soon discover if you do not learn to display appropriate behavior."

"And what is appropriate behavior? Belly-crawling to you?" She snapped the words before she really had time to consider them.

Almost the moment they left her lips, a sound like a gunshot rang out and a second later her left cheek burned fiercely. Vladimir had spanked her on the bottom, his large hand catching the entirety of her cheek.

Sacha turned on him, her lip lifted in a snarl, her anger flaring. Before she could open her mouth to address him, another hard slap landed from behind, delivered by the alpha directly to her right cheek. Alexei's swat sent her up onto her toes and forced her to scuttle out of the middle of them, both her hands fastened on her rear.

"I think it's time our newest member learned what being part of this pack means," Alexei said, rubbing his large palms together as he advanced on Sacha. She backed away from him, finding herself up against the wall, which she slid along until she backed herself in a corner in which she was quickly trapped by both alpha and beta.

They were going to punish her. They did not say a word about it, but she knew that things were about to go very, very badly for her. Both men were looking at her with a particular dominant determination that she knew was focused on one thing: her submission.

She would not give it. Sacha had not submitted ever in her life, and she was not going to begin because the scenery had changed, or because she was confronted with two dominant males. The problem was that physically she was much smaller than them. Alexei outweighed her by eighty pounds at least, and though he was less powerfully built, Vladimir was still taller and stronger than her. Either one of them would have had an advantage alone. Together, they were almost certain to get the better of her.

Sacha was left with just one choice—to shift. It happened almost without planning or thought. Her anger and her fear took animal form, her clothes sheared from her body by the force of her transformation. In seconds the slim woman was gone, and in her place was a snarling she-wolf, lips pulled back from sharp canines. She knew they could shift too, of course. In their wolf forms they could roll her over and pin her, they could fasten their jaws on her throat if they desired, they could even bite her, but they could not impart any of the humiliating punishments given to humans. As a wolf she was safe from the tumult of fear and anticipation that flooded her human body.

Alexei and Vladimir looked at one another as Sacha growled at the pair of them, her canines flashing potentially deadly warning. Now she had the power. Even a small wolf could deal lethal damage to a human with little difficulty.

Strangely, neither man seemed angry or even annoyed at her transformation. Though she was clearly a threat, they were struggling not to smile. She could see their facial muscles quirking as they worked to maintain serious demeanors.

"Oh, dear," Alexei murmured. "Look how little she is. Even for a female…"

Vladimir nodded. "They don't know how to raise wolves in England. Fish and chips and mushy peas. A weak diet that creates weak wolves. Or perhaps she was the runt."

Sacha understood every word they said through the animal filter of her mind. It was an insult to her, to her pack, to her country, to her family. Her growl grew to a feral peak and she snapped her teeth at them.

Alexei stepped forward and dealt a sharp tap to her nose. "Quiet," he ordered.

Sacha shook her head back and forth. The blow had not been painful, but it had shaken her confidence. That wasn't supposed to happen. A man should not be so casual with a wolf, even one who was a wolf himself.

She realized that she had made a mistake. They could not slap her bottom now, but becoming her wolf self had shrunk her relative stature. Alexei was even more imposing now. She found herself looking up at his much larger form and sensing his power even more keenly. As a human she had sensed it through human cues and actions, but as a wolf she could feel him on a whole new level. She was learning a great deal about this alpha, starting with the fact that he was dominant through and through. His scent filled the space, utterly undetectable to humans but potent to her animal senses. She was enveloped in him, his energy wrapped around her, holding her in an intangible yet powerful way.

"Come, Vladimir," Alexei said. "I would speak with you."

Still in her corner, Sacha watched warily as the two men turned their backs on her and walked across the room to a door at the far end. She let out a little half-growl as they opened the door and went through it, shutting it behind them to leave her to her animal devices.

• • • • • • •

Alexei had to step away. The presence of the younger female was starting to cloud his judgment. His blood was roiling in his veins and he could feel the change slipping up on him. Another second in her presence and he would have become like her. She was a provocative little minx, one who called forth the animal in him. But he was wise enough to know that human reason needed to be in play in this matter, not pure animal instinct.

"Quite a woman," Vladimir murmured in a gross understatement as the door closed behind them. "But Alexei, she does not know to behave."

"I do not think the English alpha had any control over her. She was his sister, after all. He should have sent her here decades ago," Alexei agreed. "She could have learned with the other whelps. Now she is a fully grown bitch with a taste for power... and a severe attitude problem."

"Fortunately, she is small and easily handled," Vladimir mused. "As a wolf at least..."

"We are going to have to start from the beginning with this one," Alexei frowned. "She has already proven that she is capable of shedding blood in her own pack. That cannot happen here. Subtlety will not work. She will not be subtle.

She has been here not even an hour and she has challenged the pair of us directly."

"Well, she has postured," Vladimir replied. "She was far too frightened to attack. Did you see how far her tail was tucked between her legs? Scraping her belly. She is not just aggressive. She is scared."

"So to comfort, or to punish?"

"Why not both?" Vladimir suggested. "Punishment first, comfort second."

Alexei nodded. "I will handle her alone, I think," he said. "Having both of us there is overwhelming for her."

A knowing smirk established itself on Vladimir's lips. "As you wish."

Alexei shook his head at his majordomo. "That is not what I have in mind, Vladimir."

"It is not what you have in *mind* that makes me smile," Vladimir replied.

Alexei did not dignify the comment with a response.

• • • • • • •

The door opened and only Alexei returned. Sacha had remained in wolf form, figuring it would be impossible for them to effectively handle her while she remained her beast self. Besides, her clothes were ripped and torn. She could see her panties laying pooled on the floor, ripped at the hems. There was no way she could get back into them, and there was no way she was going to display herself naked before the alpha. She slid back into the corner as he strode toward her, entirely confident.

"Back into your human state. Now." Alexei snapped the order down at her, his eyes lit with blue fire. He spoke with a growl that evoked obedience from the part of her that was beyond defiance. Sacha learned quickly that her animal self was more easily controlled than she had thought. She felt the wolf cower and start to melt away, leaving bare human flesh in its place. In seconds she was crouching naked in the corner of the room, fully human and completely embarrassed.

"Stand up." The order broke across her senses like the crack of a whip, making her wince. She did not want to stand. She did not want to move. She barely wanted to breathe.

Alexei reached down, curled his fingers in her hair, and pulled smoothly upwards. Sacha followed her hair, being rather attached to it. She ended up on her tiptoes with Alexei's hand still firmly locked in her tresses.

His eyes swept up and down her body, taking in her small breasts, her ample hips, the gentle swell of her belly, the dark pelt at the apex of her thighs, the straining length of her legs, her taut calves, her toes that just barely touched the floor thanks to his grip. She blushed furiously as she felt his eyes travel across every inch of her, taking in every curve, dimple, and freckle.

This was not how she had planned her first hour with the Russians. Caught in the alpha's grasp, Sacha realized that she had severely underestimated them—and overestimated her own abilities and general fearsomeness as well. It would have been a hard lesson to learn under any circumstances, but it was almost impossible to come to terms with while dangling naked before the alpha. An unwanted whimper rose to her lips as Alexei began to lecture her.

"You will speak with respect," he intoned. "You will obey the orders given to you by myself, Vladimir, and any other ranking pack member. You will learn the ways of our home and our family and you will be punished severely if you transgress. Do you understand?"

Yes. The word was in her head, but her pride would not allow it to come from her lips. Though she was scared, she remained silent as the alpha's eyes bored into hers.

"Speak."

The order was curt and blunt. She did not obey it. One second stretched into two and three and still she had not made any utterance other than the guttural sounds of a woman caught in a compromising position.

The tension on her hair lapsed as Alexei sat down on a nearby couch, but the grip was soon used again to haul her over his lap. She landed over hard, muscular thighs, her naked body sliding across his legs until arrested by his other arm, which coiled about her waist. Without another word, he started spanking her bottom, his palm landing with loud gunshot-like slaps that echoed through the room.

Staring down at a rich carpet, Sacha's mouth opened in a silent scream. As an onlooker, spankings had never seemed all that painful. She had thought that those who complained and whined were soft, spoiled little brats. But now that it was her own bottom being belabored she was shocked at how the spanking heated her skin immediately. Within half a dozen swats she was feeling an uncomfortable burn that spread across the surface of her cheeks at the speed of the spanking, stinging and aching and sending her senses into overdrive.

As well as the physical sensations, Sacha realized she had completely underestimated the emotional reaction. Held over Alexei's lap, she found herself locked in an undeniably intimate position. Her naked body was pressed hard against his well-made clothes and she was glad for the barrier of cloth, though it provided little in the way of modesty really. Hot embarrassment flushed her skin as her legs began to kick and the hard bud of her clit rubbed against the smooth fabric of Alexei's trousers.

Arousal was not far away, though she fought it with everything she had. If she were to become visibly wet, that would be the end of it for her. She would have no pride left at all. Sacha silently cursed herself. Taken like this, held so close to his powerful body, feeling the disparity between their size and strength, she could no longer hold onto the idea that she could somehow best him physically. He held her in place as if she weighed nothing at all, her struggles rendered void by the musculature of his arm.

The slaps fell, over and over, dozens of swats lighting

her bottom up into two hot glowing globes. At first Sacha tried to be stoic and stay completely still, acting as though she did not feel the sting or the burn or the ache that resulted from the heavier swats. But Alexei's slaps soon drove her past the point of stoicism and she could not help but vocalize her misery in muted wails that she tried her best to muffle with her hands, clapping both of them over her mouth so that her little sounds would stay a secret.

"Do you understand?"

The question was growled at her again. Again, Sacha knew that there was only one sane answer. Yes. That was all he wanted to hear. All she had to say was that one little word and the pain would be over—or surely abate. And yet she could not bring herself to say it. How could she possibly capitulate so quickly? It would be dishonor to her very bloodline to do so.

· · · · · · ·

Alexei felt the younger woman's resistance in every taut line of her gorgeous naked body. Her bottom was a bright glowing red, her soft skin ever so sensitive and responsive to the slapping of his palm.

She was brave, that much was certain. She was scared too. Scared of her new home. Scared of submission. Scared of him. And yet he could not afford to be kind. She had arrived at his home in hopes of immediately taking a position of rank. She was an entitled little brat and she needed to learn her place so he kept spanking her, his hard hand meeting her bottom with increasingly sharp slaps that served to make her cheeks bounce and jiggle in a pleasing fashion. She had a very nice body, not the body of a very young woman, but one with maturity in the hips and thighs. She was fit, but soft where she should be soft.

He had an impulse to spread her thighs and bury his face between her legs where the dark covering of feminine fur hid a place of mutual delight, but that too would spoil her.

Alexei had known many women who used sex to control. But that did not seem like Sacha's style. She was not a seductress. If anything, she was slightly awkward in a charming fashion. Her nudity had embarrassed her; he had seen that much. And yet even now that she squirmed and made muffled little sounds of despair over his thighs, he could scent her desire.

Her body knew what she needed to do, but her stubborn mind was making her tender flesh suffer for pride's sake.

"Sacha. Do you understand?" He snapped the words in harsh tones, making his accent thick and authoritarian at the same time. He felt her quiver in response, but she stayed silent.

He pushed her thighs apart and landed a slap directly on the soft flesh between her legs, catching her lower lips under his fingers.

She jolted and let out a shriek uninhibited by restraint. That had shocked her. He saw her hips grind down against his leg in a quick reaction that he could have missed if he were not watching her so carefully. He smirked darkly, realizing that Sacha did not just need firm handling—she desired it.

· · · · · · ·

With the alpha's slap burning across her pussy lips, Sacha was thrown into a world of shock and pain. She could not believe what had happened. Worse still, when she tried to close her thighs he made a grunting sound in the negative, parted them again, and laid yet another sharp slap to her pussy.

Her legs held apart, her cunt exposed to the alpha's gaze, Sacha began to whimper almost nonstop. There were no words capable of adequately protesting this treatment. She was being punished in a thoroughly humiliating fashion and there was nothing she could do about it.

Alexei started his spanking again, landing a swat to each

cheek and then one between her thighs. He did it slowly, methodically, so she knew the one between her legs was coming and almost welcomed the slaps to her bottom because at least they meant that a stinging slap was not making her pussy lips swell with heat, a physical reaction she could not control.

"You're wet."

Two words that did not demand she swear her obedience to him, and yet she wished that instead he had asked her yet again if she understood. That would have been better than the verbal acknowledgment of her shameful reaction to his discipline.

His fingers grazed lightly over her lower lips, teasing her. She did not know what to make of that touch, which would have been nice if it were not being given on a well spanked pussy. Sacha gasped as he cupped her sex and squeezed gently in a possessive gesture that made her emit a small moan. The tips of his fingers were pressing against her clit, grinding gently as he started massaging her between her legs with little circular motions. The friction against her punished pussy wasn't entirely without pain. She let out little hisses and gasps, but there were more moans too as he moved his hand faster and faster in those little circles, pinching her clit between two of his fingers so the little bud was stimulated with every motion.

Having her pussy spanked and then rubbed was enough to make her tired, overstimulated body rush into the throes of a quick, hard, and limb-trembling orgasm. Sacha screamed as she came with his hand pressed over her pussy, her red bottom jiggling with the motion as he used his grasp between her thighs to lift her off his lap a little, putting the pressure of her weight against her sensitive slit.

Alexei gave her little time to recover from the experience. Sacha was still quivering with the aftershocks of pleasure as he stood her up between his thighs and looked her in the eye. Her gaze dipped a little lower, to where a long, thick erection was tenting the front of his pants. Her climax had left her wet, but not entirely sated. There was a new tension as they looked at one another differently than before. Sacha no longer felt like so much of an outcast—and she no longer felt as though she were so very far from home.

"Do you understand now?" He asked the question one more time, his accent thick with lust.

She looked at him and shook her head. "No."

Alexei lifted the corner of his mouth in a snarl and stood up. Sacha squealed as his leg hooked around hers and she was tipped back onto the rug. He guided her to the floor, his legs between her knees. She knew what was going to happen now. Sex was in the air. Her legs spread willingly as he covered her body with his, his lips on hers, his tongue snaking into her mouth. His cock was freed from his pants and the thick head found her sore, spanked slit unerringly, pushing into the slick wetness in one easy thrust.

Fucked on the floor of the alpha's office, Sacha grasped at his shoulders, her legs wrapped around his powerful waist as he drove deep inside her. There was something urgent in his eyes, a primal animal impulse that matched her own desire. This was madness. He was a stranger to her and yet her body was welcoming him as if it had been waiting for him forever. Her pussy wrapped around his cock, her natural lubrication making his shaft gleam as it slid in and out of her over and over again. Her lips were sensitive from the spanking he had given them, but it was not pain she felt, rather another string to the symphony of sensation rising in her.

He fucked her as if he were dying of thirst and she were the only water in the world. There was tremendous desire and passion in his touch, his kiss, the way he let his hands roam over her body, pinching her nipples as he slid his cock home and ground himself against her, pubic bone meeting pubic bone.

With the initial frenzy of sexual conquest over, slowly he began to settle into something of a less frantic rhythm. He held himself still inside her and kissed her deeply, wrapping one hand in her hair to hold her in place as his mouth ravaged hers. Sacha made little humping motions with her hips, working herself on his hard shaft. She slid easily on his cock, her wetness growing with every passing thrust. She was as hungry for him as he seemed to be for her, and when she started to whimper from not being allowed the longer strokes, he soon came to her aid and pulled out to the very tip then sank all the way in, sliding inside her with an almost torturous slowness.

It was a rhythm neither of them could stand for very long. Sacha's pussy was clenched and tight as her clit hardened to a little pebble of need. The slower and longer he fucked her, the more she felt her orgasm building—and soon she could feel him pulsing inside her, his cock growing larger than she had thought possible.

"I'm going to come," he groaned against her ear. "I'm going to come inside you, Sacha."

Come inside you. The words flipped a switch in Sacha's brain and body. Almost instantly a hard climax washed over her, an orgasm unlike any she had given herself with desperate rubbing that had passed for masturbation. This was an entirely different feeling, something that swept over her body and held her in thrall for stroke after stroke as Alexei growled against her neck and did his best to prolong their lovemaking for what seemed like an eternity.

Sacha wailed and thrashed about under him, her puffy pussy lips red and swollen around his hardness as he picked up the pace in the final stampede, lifted her legs high and pounded her coming pussy until he let out a roar of triumph and locked his hips against her ass, spending himself deep inside her cunt. He held himself there, his semen filling her to the very brim, before slowly pulling out, bringing a trickle of cum with him.

He heard her little whimper of pain as he slid from her body and frowned. "I hurt you."

"You didn't hurt me," Sacha said. "That was just…

intense…"

With a small grunt of acknowledgment, Alexei pulled a blanket from over the back of a chair and wrapped it around her shoulders, pulling her to sit between his legs.

Tinged with affection and post-coital warmth, his dominance was not quite so hard to accept. His arm slid around her waist and he pulled her against his body, his long legs on either side of her as he cradled her against his torso. For long minutes they stared wordlessly into the leaping flames in the grate.

"It has been a very long time since I have lain with a woman," he said at length.

Those words surprised Sacha. Alexei did not seem to her to be a man who would have to look very far for female companionship. "You must have many eager females vying to be your mate."

"Eagerness is not sufficient qualification to take a place in my bed, let alone by my side, let alone become the dominant female of this pack," he said, gently reminding her in the process that sex alone did not a mate make. He had fucked her, yes, but that didn't necessarily mean anything to him—though it meant everything to her.

Sacha lowered her eyes from the flames to the embers and tried not to let her disappointment show. It should have been easy enough given he could only see the very top of her head, but somehow she gave herself away.

"I am saying you are special," he said gently, sensing the shift in her energies. "Though you should not take that as a sign that I have assigned you rank in this pack."

"I am still the lowest of the low," Sacha said, her tone somewhere between bitterness and playfulness. "I am not worthy even to gather the crumbs from under your table…" She let out a little yelp as his teeth once more grazed the back of her neck before fastening swiftly in a quick, punitive nip.

"You will need many lessons in modulating your tone," he said as she squirmed, her aching bottom still sore from the spanking he had delivered. "I will not tolerate attitude, Sacha."

She smiled into the flames. For all his warnings and all his lectures and all his spankings, she knew that she had made some impression on him. He had lost control and in doing so spent himself inside her. That counted for something. Perhaps for everything. As her mind slid back to the memory of their mating, she yet again saw his face as he entered her. His handsome features had been a mask of pure need. He hadn't made love to her because it was the right and proper thing to do. He had done it because pure animal passion had dictated it to both of them. She had no doubt that Alexei ran his pack with an iron paw, but he had his weaknesses. Beneath the hard, formal exterior was a man of great passion. That was the key.

"What to do with you now," he said, musing to himself. "I certainly cannot put you with the other females, they will scent my seed on you and be jealous."

Sacha's smirk grew a little wider. Her plan to gain rank in the pack, which had seemed to go so very awry when she was naked over his lap, now seemed to be falling perfectly into place. Alexei might not be making her his mate, but she was covered in his scent and everyone in the pack would know it. She had but to walk through the house and the fact of their coupling would be common knowledge within minutes.

"I can sense your devious thoughts," he chided her. "You would gladly display yourself, wouldn't you."

"I am a modest woman," Sacha said formally. "I have no interest in causing unrest in this place."

"Oh, what a little liar you are," he laughed. "You are an agent of chaos, Sacha. I know that much. I do not think you will be ready to be released into the pack until I have you well in hand. No. I will keep you as mine. My little pet."

"Pet?" Her upper lip curled with the word. "Must you degrade me so?"

"It is not a term of degradation, but endearment," Alexei

corrected her. "It is an honor. And I can assure you, it is better than the alternative."

"Which is?"

"I give you to Vladimir and he takes his cane to you until such time as he considers you properly chastised. I think that time would be a long way off where you are concerned."

Sacha shivered involuntarily. Alexei was fearsome in many respects, but where his passion ran hot, Vladimir was stone cold. She could easily see herself ending up in a world of pain if she were to be left to the beta's tender mercies.

"Come," Alexei said. "Let us bathe together."

• • • • • • •

The luxury of the alpha's quarters was apparent everywhere, but especially in the bathroom. The tub was as big as a small swimming pool. Large enough that she could quite easily let her feet rise to the surface of the water and simply float in circles.

"It is heated by an underground spring," Alexei murmured as he watched her laze in the water, answering a question she had not asked.

He stripped his clothing off, revealing a body that was muscular and toned. Sacha looked at him boldly, taking in every part of him with interest and hunger.

A large scar ran from his left pectoral almost to his belly button. Sacha knew that kind of wound. It was of the kind that would have been inflicted when he was in wolf form, pinned on his back and attacked viciously. It was the kind of wound designed to tear the guts out of an animal. She stared at it, unable to fathom the creature that could have inflicted that much damage on Alexei.

"I have fought for my position too," he said with a smile that made her blush as it made reference to the reason for her exile.

"But you were successful where I was not."

He smiled sympathetically as he slid into the water. "We all lose at some point, pet."

"Have you lost?"

"I lost many times before I won."

"So you're saying I should keep fighting."

"Not unless you want scars like mine," he said, running his hands over her naked body in a slow caress. "I would not want these for you, pet."

She let out a small growl as he used that little word again, the one that made her feel small and if she were to admit it, warm as well. His arms wrapped around her waist, further emphasizing the difference in their size and strength as he pulled her back against his body and sat on the inner ledge of the bath with her sore bottom propped on his thigh, the pressure mercifully alleviated somewhat by the buoyancy of being in water.

The intimacy was intoxicating. Sacha found her head descending against his shoulder as the warmth of the water made her muscles relax. It had been a very long, very strange, very curious journey from England to the alpha's bath and she found herself left with more questions than answers.

Alexei began to wash her, running a lathered cloth over her skin in long languid strokes, which further served to lull her into submission. She was floating in the arms of the only alpha to ever have her carnally, his scent all over her in spite of the water lapping around her breasts and shoulders. She could taste him on her lips and her aching nethers pulsed constant reminders of their lovemaking. The ache in her bottom was also present, another reminder of his dominion over her. By any objective measure, she had been conquered.

But Sacha did not feel conquered. She felt cosseted and adored. There was care in his touch as he used massaging motions to soothe away both the aches of her muscles and the grime of long haul air travel. For long minutes she was silent, basking in the sheer pleasure of being pampered after so much turmoil. The fear that had been coiled in her stomach from the moment Lorcan had declared she was to be sent into exile—and perhaps had been there long before that announcement had been made—was starting to unwind. What fear could there be in the arms of a man like Alexei?

The spell was not broken until they left the bath. Alexei dried her as carefully as he had washed her, patting every part of her dry, even her sore rear, which he paid tender attention to before wrapping her in a large soft towel that made her feel secure and gave her some semblance of modesty. He led her from the bathroom into his bedchamber, a room so large it made her feel small all over again. The bed was of an impressive size that certainly did not conform to traditional expectations. Six or seven people could probably have a comfortable night's sleep in the behemoth.

"You should hear the girls complain at the size of the sheets," Alexei said, his cheek dimpling as he caught her looking at the bed.

The girls. The ones upstairs, the ones she would have been put with if not for her insistence on immediately meeting the alpha. Sacha's lips twisted at the ludicrous idea of being a maidservant in this great house. That was not her style or her station. It was far more appropriate for her to be here with the naked alpha, freshly mated. Yes. Sacha felt a deep sense of satisfaction spreading through her as she realized she had more than achieved the goal she'd had at the outset.

She was pleased with how things were now going, though one question still lingered in her mind. "The men who picked me up," she said. "The turnip transporters. Did you send them on purpose?"

"Vladimir handled your transportation," Alexei replied. "Was it not to your liking?"

She saw the way his cheek muscle quirked as he replied. That was all it took to let her know that it had absolutely been planned.

"It didn't work out as you had planned, did it," she smirked up at him. "I am not so easily humiliated, Alexei."

"No? Well, I will enjoy finding ways to make you blush, my pet," he murmured, brushing his lips over the top of her head in a tender kiss the spirit of which seemed to run contrary to his words. "I know you are far from tame yet, Sacha."

"I cannot be tamed, Alexei. It is not in my blood," she replied. Her attempt to move away from him was halted quickly by his hand encircling the back of her neck, fingers pinching lightly but hard enough for her to feel the strength of his direction.

"I think you can be tamed, Sacha," he growled softly in her ear. "More than that, I think you want to be."

His words made her clit pulse and her hips squirm. This was new to Sacha. Never before had she met a man so capable of turning her to liquid. The stoic, cold exterior she always projected had no chance of standing up against the intensity of his dominance. She could feel the hard ridge of muscular thigh beneath her legs, the equally unyielding plane of his stomach and chest pressed against the soft curves of her body. And then there was his gaze. She wasn't looking at him and yet she could feel his eyes on her.

"You're blushing now," he observed. "That was easy."

Sacha let out a little sound of complaint, not a word, but something closer to a whine that turned to a growl as he tipped her head to the side and grazed his teeth down the side of her neck in a possessive, hungry gesture.

He chuckled at her complaint, turned and began casting through a drawer of jewelry that looked like the proceeds of some dramatic movie heist. There was so much wealth in one small space that for a moment she was quite taken aback. Her own pack was well to do, but there was no hint of this kind of opulence at Darkwood Manor. Alexei sorted through priceless heirlooms with a casual demeanor that spoke to being accustomed to a much higher standard of living than she had ever been fortunate enough to experience. Again her excitement peaked as she started to realize just how she had fallen on her feet. This was not an exile. This was a reward. She cast her eye over the drawer of jewels and all the other drawers and cabinets and displayed pieces and realized that she was about to be rich beyond her wildest dreams.

Oh, what she would do then. Her lips curled back from her teeth as she thought about returning to Darkwood Manor in triumph. She might even buy it and cast Lorcan and his whore bride out. Adrenaline and the prospect of revenge made her excitement rise all the more

"Let us talk terms, my pet," Alexei said, picking up what looked to Sacha like a heavy gold choker.

"Terms?" She had no idea what he was talking about. She had been so caught up in her fantasies of reclaiming the manor that she had utterly forgotten there was some purpose to Alexei's actions.

"I cannot have you roaming these halls unattended," he said, his blue eyes capturing her attention. "I cannot trust your obedience, for I do not think you have any, and I cannot trust you to keep the peace, because I think you would cause chaos at the first opportunity. Every untamed pet needs a handler. I would assign you to Vladimir, but I think you are too sensitive for him…"

Sacha let out a little choked sound, somewhere between relief and offense. "You think me sensitive?"

"Oh, you are very sensitive, Sacha. Every part of you responds to the lightest touch. Your skin is soft and unaccustomed to work or punishment. You require a particular kind of handling."

He spoke as if he knew her intimately, when in reality they had only known one another for a matter of an hour. A blush rose to Sacha's cheeks as he spoke to her in those dominant, but somehow soft tones, reading her soul aloud.

"So, you see, you must be my pet," he said. "And I must tell you my terms so you will not cause yourself more grief than is necessary."

Sacha still bridled at the term 'pet,' but she knew she would not get a closer position to the alpha. To reject his offer outright would probably be to consign herself to a dungeon, or to the less than tender ministrations of the majordomo. "Very well," she said as proudly as any woman could speak while her spanked bottom was covered only by a towel. "What are your terms?"

Alexei beckoned her closer with one crooked finger. She took a step toward him and stood still as he draped the jewelry around her.

"You will wear my collar," he said, fastening the choker around her neck. "You will not take your wolf form, under any circumstances, without my permission. You will sleep at the foot of my bed and you will obey my every order. At mealtimes you will eat by my side, or from a bowl on the floor if you have displeased me or broken any of the rules of the pack."

Sacha felt outrage rising further with every word he said.

"Never," she spat. "Never will I eat from the floor. You must be utterly mad to think that you could ask such a thing of me, let alone command it!"

His face grew hard. All traces of his previous kind demeanor evaporated. When he spoke again his voice was harsh and his accent seemed thicker than before.

"You are too proud, Sacha. You have been spoiled. You have been coddled. It has not done you any good. I am not your brother and I will not repeat his mistakes."

Alexei's eyes had become cold and his bearing unyielding. He stood much taller than her and Sacha took a step back to give him the full benefit of her withering stare. He could thrash her. He could fuck her. He could take her clothes from her, but he would not break her pride.

"My brother's mistake was in thinking that he could export his problems. Your mistake is thinking that you can change me."

• • • • • • •

His little pet was being very naughty and very defiant, but Alexei could not help being somewhat impressed as she stood before him, every part of her being filled with pride. Even with her hair wet and bedraggled, her body clad in nothing more than a towel, she was almost regal.

Alexei's desire flared as he watched her do her very best to impose her will on him. She had no idea how her attitude inflamed his ardor, how her resistance made her all the more desirable.

He reached out, grasped the front of her towel, and pulled her to him, her toes leaving the floor for a moment as his lips crushed hers in a passionate kiss. Her mouth opened, probably in some kind of complaint, but it allowed his tongue to enter her mouth and silence her for a brief moment.

Alexei felt her flesh quiver against his, her instinct to submit rising inside her. She couldn't help her physical reaction, what her body told her was the right thing to do, to allow him to take charge, to follow him in all things. But equally her spirit remained rebellious and he could feel that too, the flame that drew him over and over again even though he knew he was dancing with danger. Sacha was not merely an impulsive little brat. She was potentially a dominant bitch—and he had seen enough in his lifetime to know how much damage one of those could do in a very short period of time.

She would think his collar and rules were cruel, but in truth they were absolutely necessary not only to maintain order, but to have her become a part of his pack. He tugged at the towel and it fell from her body, leaving her beautiful naked form bared to his gaze.

"On your knees."

He knew she would refuse the order, just as she must have known he would not allow her to refuse it. When she remained standing in defiant fashion, he reached out, took a thick handful of her hair, and pressed her down with gentle but relentless force until she sank down and took to her knees on the floor before him.

Alexei held her in place, her lips just inches from his cock.

"Suck me, pet."

She growled her defiance, but when he pushed the hardening head of his rod against her lips she did not resist him. Her mouth opened to allow him entrance to her yet again, her hot, wet, soft mouth becoming the vessel of his pleasure just as her tight pussy had been.

Yellow eyes met his blue ones as he pushed himself as deep as he could go without making her gag, the underside of his cock sliding over her tongue. There was still rebellion in those eyes; no matter how he made her submit, her spirit remained.

Not that he wanted to break her, of course, he just wanted to see her waver. He wanted to sense that moment when the facade she projected so convincingly began to crack and she let him in as her master. It was perhaps too soon for that. For the moment he would content himself with obedience and with the delicious softness of her mouth, her tongue lapping around his cock as she made what seemed almost like instinctive motions with her mouth. Some part of her wanted this, of that he had no doubt.

Just as he was beginning to believe she was submitting to him, he felt her teeth brush against his rod, a little too much to be accidental.

"Careful," he murmured, tightening his grip in her hair. "You don't want to be punished, do you, Sacha?"

She growled around his cock, sending vibrations through his flesh. It was time to put an end to this defiance. He kept his grip tight and began thrusting his hips back and forth more forcefully, taking her with a determined dominance that made the most of her mouth. Little wet sounds escaped her as he came a second time, spending himself over her tongue and down her throat. Not a drop was spilled, and he noted that she made no attempt to spit or otherwise reject his cum. If anything she seemed to savor it, her eyes narrowing ever so slightly in a way that was more cunning than angry.

His seed was now in her belly and between her thighs. She was full of his essence, a fact that seemed to please her. Alexei had the strangest feeling that the more he dominated this little witch of a woman, the more powerful she felt herself to be.

A growl from her stomach changed the direction of his thoughts.

"You must be famished," he said, frowning. "What kind of a host am I?"

Sacha wiped her mouth on the back of her hand before replying. "The best. The kind who has a guest thrown into a van, and then makes use of her body as a sexual amusement."

He raised a brow at her dry sarcasm. Even with her rear hot and sore, her pussy freshly fucked, and her mouth no doubt ripe with the taste of his seed, she remained defiant. Something like excitement stirred inside him as he contemplated what it might take to make her understand her place—but that could wait. She needed food.

Alexei ordered a meal from the kitchen, which was delivered in short order. In the meantime, he provided her with a black silk robe and bade her sit on the bed. She would not be allowed to sleep on it, but it was the softest place for a sore bottom to rest.

When the meal came, he saw the hunger in her eyes. If he were to be absolutely strict about matters, this first meal was the most important in terms of establishing order. He should have made her sit and ask nicely, take it from his fingers or from the floor—that would have taught her several lessons in one fell swoop—and yet he could not quite bring himself to do it. Perhaps he was enjoying her spirit and fire more than he could admit to himself.

At any rate, he let her eat without interference. There would be time to train her in the manners of a pet. For the moment he wanted her nourished. She was very pale, perhaps because of her natural complexion, more likely from exhaustion. Her proud inner fire made it easy to forget just how very far she was from home, and under what circumstances she had arrived. She was a woman alone in the world—and all she had was him.

CHAPTER FOUR

It felt good to be full. Sacha had not eaten properly since Lorcan had announced that she was to be exiled. Days had passed since her belly had been sated and the meats and vegetables delivered by Lorcan's chef called to her with a voice that would not be denied. The portions were generous and she consumed all there was, fearing that if things were not to go well she may not eat again for some time.

It struck her as strange that she was relaxed enough to eat in the company of a man who had made her his sexual plaything, who had not only seduced her, but made use of her mouth as a means of demonstrating his power. Alexei made her feel many things: anger, outrage, arousal… and, apparently, safety. It was his presence, his calm, certain dominance that soothed her animal soul.

"It is bedtime, pet," he said once she had eaten. "You will sleep here," he continued, pointing to a bearskin rug at the foot of the bed.

Sacha's lips curled into a sneer. "On the floor? Do not tell me you were serious about that lunacy."

He answered by pulling her up from the bed and slapping her bottom sharply. "You are my pet. Pets sleep at the foot of their master's bed."

The collar necklace around her throat seemed heavier in that moment, a weight of humiliation as she realized he truly meant what he had said. She was to be treated with no more accord than an animal—and not a wild wolf, but a domesticated little pet.

Every moment with Alexei brought with it new pleasures and fresh humiliations. First a spanking, then sex, then a bath, then being taken to her knees and having her mouth used for his pleasure, then food, and now the expectation that she would curl up on a rug and go to sleep like a tired pup.

The worst thing about it was that with food in her belly and the adrenaline from her arrival starting to dissipate, she was starting to feel very, very tired. The bed looked like the most comfortable thing in the universe. She craved it.

"Sit down on the rug," Alexei ordered gently.

She slumped down as her energy waned and watched with wide, tired eyes as he took one of the many pillows from the bed, as well as a comforter. The pillow he put next to her on the rug, then pointed at it.

"Lie down."

What choice was there but to obey? Sacha slid down and put her head on the pillow, trying to maintain as much dignity as was possible in such a situation. Fortunately for her, the floor was not as hard as she thought it would be. There must have been something under the bearskin, because she felt her body sink into it in a way that it would not on a hard floor. The fur was warm and comforting and lying on it was not at all as strange as she thought it would be. If she had been in her wolf form, she would probably have spent long minutes rolling around on it, luxuriating in the softness. Her human inhibitions meant that all she did was run her fingers through the fur as Alexei arranged the blanket over her. There was care in his touch, and comfort too.

Sacha had not been put to bed in a very, very long time. Her mind was taken back to a time when she was not the most dominant female in the pack, when she was small and cherished and taken care of in every way. She had quite forgotten what it felt like to be treated like that.

"Sleep well, pet," Alexei said, turning out the light and leaving her in warm darkness in which sleep was waiting to receive her.

• • • • • • •

It was much later in the evening when Alexei went to bed. It was strange for there to be another living soul in the room, even though she was silent and curled up at the foot of the bed, fast asleep. It had been a very long time since he had allowed any woman in his bedroom. He would have to be careful about the exceptions he was making for the little Englishwoman. Still, he could admit to himself that it was nice to feel another presence in the room as he slipped between the sheets and went to sleep.

Hours later, Alexei woke to a low wailing and sniffling. At first he was thoroughly confused, then he remembered Sacha. She was crying to herself.

"Pet?"

She made no reply, but the crying sound became quieter. The sobs turned to little sniffles interjected with bigger gasps where she lost control of her misery.

Alexei sighed inwardly. As much discipline as Sacha needed, he could not lie there and listen to her weep through the night.

"Come here, pet."

When she did not move he got up, scooped her up from the floor, and took her into the bed with him. His resolve was crumbling where she was concerned all too quickly, but he was not entirely without compassion and he could not leave her to cry on the floor.

She was stiff at first, resistant to his comfort, but the longer he held her the more she softened in his arms. The tears that she tried to restrain started to flow again as he rubbed her back and her hip and her thighs, caressing her body in long, soothing strokes.

"It is difficult, being so far from home," he murmured against her ear. "And these rules are not easy to follow, but I will take care of you, my pet."

Sacha did not say anything in response, but the sobs that shook her body began to lessen and eventually trail off completely. Almost all of the rules he had formulated for her had been broken, but that didn't seem to matter compared to the warmth he felt in his chest as he held her soft curves against his body. He would put her back at the end of the bed when she had settled, but a few more minutes wouldn't hurt.

Just... a... few... more... his eyelids grew heavier and his breathing began to slow and before Alexei was truly aware of his own tiredness they were both fast asleep, Sacha wrapped securely in his arms, her head nestled under his chin and an expression of pure contentment on both their faces.

CHAPTER FIVE

For three days Alexei kept Sacha contained in his quarters and neither of them were seen by the pack at large. In his rooms they made love time and time again, exhausting one another with a shared lust that seemed more powerful than either of them. He treated her as a pet, but a spoiled, cosseted one. After the very first hours of the first night she did not sleep on the floor, she slept curled in his arms—and she certainly never ate from the floor.

The honeymoon, such as it was, could not last forever. Soon Alexei announced that he had business to attend to and that she was free to amuse herself on the floor on which his quarters were located, the main feature of which was a grand library that was more like a museum than a traditional library. The history of the pack was contained there in leather-bound tomes and glass cases and lined shelves that reached far above Sacha's head.

It must have been his thinking that there was little in the way of trouble for her to get into, but trouble soon found her.

Sacha was sitting by herself in the great library when three women approached her. There were not many other people around on Alexei's floor, so Sacha was surprised to see the single women who almost certainly should not have been there. There was tall blonde perhaps half a decade younger than Sacha, flanked by mousier, shorter females who Sacha did not bother to pay any mind to because it was the one in the center from whom hostility flowed like wine.

Sacha rose to her feet as the women stopped before her, each of them giving her an unfriendly stare. Something about their demeanor told her that she did not want to be caught sitting down for this meeting.

"You're the Englishwoman," the woman said, saying the word 'Englishwoman' as if it were the most vile curse word she could imagine.

"I am," Sacha said calmly. She kept her features composed as the younger woman looked her up and down. She was quite a beauty, pale blue eyes and flowing gold locks that must have been washed and dried and curled just that morning. Her makeup was done with equal attention to glamor. Her skin was flawless, perfect porcelain pale with a hint of color in the contour of her cheeks. This was a woman who brought men to her knees. And for some reason, she seemed very angry at Sacha.

"My name is Svetlana," the woman introduced herself in cold tones. "And I will say this only once. Stay away from Alexei. He is not to be soiled by foreign blood."

Sacha mused silently over how sad it was that this confrontation should be taking place over a man. This Svetlana clearly did not know of the humiliating arrangement that kept Sacha close to Alexei. His gold collar was hidden beneath a silk scarf, which gave Sacha some sense of dignity in the face of the pack at large.

As Sacha remained silent, Svetlana took a step forward, lifted her nose, and took in a deep breath of air.

"I can smell him on you," she declared, the color draining from her painted skin, leaving her with a mask of cosmetics. "You have been touching him. How dare you!"

Sacha's dark brow rose slowly as the woman who moments ago had been a total stranger, started to work herself into what could only be described as a frenzy. Her displeasure was mirrored in the faces of her friends, whose eyes narrowed and mouths flattened to angry sneers at the realization that yes, Sacha smelled as though she had taken an Alexei bath.

"You have no right to him," Svetlana said. "He is mine. I was born to be his bride. Everybody knows it."

"I suppose I did not receive the message," Sacha replied in dry English tones, which only served to further infuriate the pretty Svetlana. "And, for that matter, nor did he."

Svetlana let out a little laugh of pure outrage. "Alexei has been chaste since the death of his mate. We were waiting for the time of his mourning to pass. It is I who has been chosen for him. I who will replace Katya."

That was news to Sacha, though now she thought about it, she supposed it made perfect sense. Alexei was not the sort of man who would ever want for female company and yet he seemed to have preferred solitude prior to her arrival.

"He was married?"

"Ha, see how little you know of him? How little you know of us?" Svetlana sneered, her beautiful features becoming ugly. "Katya was his childhood sweetheart. They married when they were both eighteen. She died seven years later."

"And he has not taken a mate since? That is a very long mourning period," Sacha noted dryly. "How patient you must be."

"There is no need for patience when one knows one's destiny," Svetlana replied. "I am meant for him, and he is meant for me."

"Well," Sacha said with a slight shrug. "Perhaps you should inform him of this fact. I can assure you I have never heard him mention your name…"

Hot color came rushing back to Svetlana's face as rage began to consume her. Sacha could see that this was a woman in love, perhaps delusionally so, but still, her feelings were very real—as was her hostility. Sacha didn't need to look around to know that she was alone with this little pack of angry women. They had made sure to come when she was separate, so whatever they did they would do without witnesses. All her senses told her that there was danger. She could smell it, she could feel it in the prickling of the rising hairs on the back of her neck, and she saw it written in Svetlana's gaze. She was looking at a woman who intended on defending her man at all costs—regardless of the fact that he had no obvious interest in her whatsoever.

Sacha felt her own anger rising. How dare they take her for some weakling to be intimidated. She was not at all intimidated by Svetlana or her little cronies.

"He is mine," Svetlana hissed again. "Stay away from him."

Sacha's lips rose into a cold smile. What Svetlana wanted, she'd already had so many times it felt as though Alexei were branded upon her.

"How fascinating," Sacha said in deceptively conversational tones. "It did not seem to me that he was yours when his cock was deep inside me." She spoke graphically on purpose, wanting to wound the woman with the facts of the matter.

Three separate shrieks of shock and outrage met her declaration. A split-second later, sharp fingernails raked a bloody trail across Sacha's nose and cheek as Svetlana lost her temper and went on the offensive, attacking Sacha with feminine fury.

This was not the fight Sacha had expected. She had expected the bitch to shift and become wolf and settle things properly. Instead she found herself engaging in a strangely futile conflict. Instead of teeth and claws, it was nails and hair pulling, tedious perhaps, but not in any way mortally dangerous.

Before Svetlana could land another slashing blow, Sacha reached out, grabbed the blond locks, and kicked Svetlana's legs out from under her. Together they went to the floor in a mass of hair and flowing fabric. Svetlana had already lost.

Sacha had no intention of letting the bitch get away with drawing blood, and now she had her on the floor the fight was hers to win. She maneuvered atop Svetlana's squirming form, pinning the Russian to the floor and prepared to unleash a special kind of havoc on her attacker.

Svetlana would surely have been taught a lesson, but for the swishing sound that heralded a bamboo cane slicing through the air. The length of it made harsh contact with her ass, emitting a sound like a gunshot. For a second, Sacha felt nothing, then suddenly hot hell blazed across her ass with enough intensity to make her let go.

The stroke was followed with a boomed command: "Enough!"

Sacha looked up to see that Vladimir stood over the pair of them, long cane in his hand. He was looking at her with an indignant fury that seemed to be focused solely on her person. In an instant, Sacha knew that it was she who was to be blamed for this altercation. With that being the case, she decided she may as well earn the punishment she knew she was to receive. She turned back to grab hold of Svetlana again, but Vladimir's distraction had allowed the blonde a chance to whimper and crawl away. She was now cowering in the arms of her friends, crocodile tears flowing as she played the perfect victim.

Far from cowering, Sacha rose to her feet and faced him directly, keeping her ass out of the line of further fire.

"You both know better than this," Vladimir growled. "Fighting is not tolerated in this house. You have disgraced yourselves and you will pay the price."

Thin streaks of blood were starting to congeal on Sacha's cheeks, scratches left by Svetlana's cruel talons. She could feel them as she started to speak.

"This little whore wanted to fight because she has some delusional notion that the alpha belongs in her bed," Sacha said. "This was not my fight. I did not start it."

Svetlana was still cowering and whimpering on the floor, making out as if she had been seriously hurt. Sacha knew better. Svetlana was not hurt in the least bit, but she was going to play the victim card hard. The worst thing about it was that it worked.

"I'm sorry," Svetlana whimpered. "I am so sorry. I have disgraced myself and this house…"

"Go to the nurse, Svetlana," Vladimir ordered. "Have her assess and tend to your injuries." His dark eyes swept back to Sacha. "You will come with me."

"What injuries! I did not have a chance to touch her," Sacha exclaimed. "I am the one with blood on my face. Do you not want my injuries assessed?"

Dark eyes ran over her dispassionately. "You have a few scratches," he said in that hard accent so native to his people. "I will leave more painful marks when I am done with you."

"Well, there's my incentive to go with you," Sacha pointed out, her tone laced with derisive sarcasm. Her body was still flooded with adrenaline and she had no intention of letting Vladimir punish her for something that was not her fault.

Vladimir reached out and took the lobe of her ear between his thumb and his forefinger, squeezing hard enough to send pain shooting through the extremity. He twisted just hard enough to make her squeal, then marched her from the scene of the scuffle through the house to his private offices, which were not nearly as large or well-appointed as Alexei's.

"Take me to Alexei and let him deal with me," Sacha appealed.

"The alpha has more important business than dealing with fights between low-ranking bitches," Vladimir replied coldly. "Lift the hem of that dress and bend over the desk."

"No," Sacha refused flatly.

Vladimir took hold of her again. He was clearly adept in the art of handling recalcitrant subordinates because as much as she squirmed and fought she found herself pressed down over an austere desk, her dress tossed up over her back with no ceremony whatsoever. The majordomo put his hand on her lower back, pinning her in place as he brought the cane down in six hard, fast strokes that whipped through the air and cracked against her bare cheeks in swift succession.

The punishment was over before she really registered it as having happened, but the moment he let her up she put her hands back to her burning, welted, bruised bottom and jumped up, swearing and cursing a storm. Each and every stroke of the cane had made a painful impression on the tissue beneath the skin and fat that made her soft rounds so appealing. Unlike a hand spanking, which heated the skin and made her senses tingle, the cane affected every layer of her being. Skin, fat, muscle, it was all impacted by the harsh stroke of the heavy bamboo. Though the caning itself had not lasted more than thirty seconds, Sacha knew she would be feeling its effects for several days.

Vladimir watched her dispassionately, his arms crossed over his chest as she exclaimed in pain, unable to breathe properly for all her exclamations. She had to stop swearing just to take a deep breath, which only made the soreness in her ass seem to swell.

"You're a vicious bastard and I'm going to kill you," she snarled at him, her temper getting the better of her.

His expression did not change in the slightest. "Do you want another six strokes?"

"No!"

"Then get out of here and compose yourself," he said coldly.

His demeanor aside, Sacha knew it was a merciful response. He could have taken the cane to her again, he could have beaten her black and blue. Instead he was letting her run away and lick her wounds. She was smart enough to take the opportunity before he changed his mind.

• • • • • •

Sacha fled to the bedroom and flung herself upon Alexei's bed. He was not there, and she was glad for it as she sobbed into the sheets, putting on a display of feminine weakness that would have shamed her had anyone been around to witness it.

She had never felt so homesick as she did then. Back at home in Darkwood no female would have dared attack her. This pack was full of brutes and she did not have an ally among them. She was utterly alone and at the mercy of those who would do her harm.

Her tears soon soaked the coverlet under her cheek, tears she bitterly resented crying, but could not help. Utter misery and dismay had overcome her and she was their joint prisoner. Even the thought of revenge did not cheer her up. There would be revenge, certainly, that Sacha promised herself. But equally she knew she would likely cause herself more pain in the process. Svetlana was smart enough to mask her aggression when others were around, and Sacha had not made any kind of impression upon her. The bitch had not submitted and had certainly not been punished.

Sacha had to admit to herself that she had been defeated. It may even have been Svetlana's plan all along to cause enough of a disturbance that Vladimir would find them. Intentional or not, there was no doubt that Sacha bore far more pain than the treacherous blonde.

She heard Alexei enter the room and curled up more tightly around herself. She could not bear another lecture and more punishment, though she was certain both would soon come her way. His step was purposeful and she could feel his energy even at a distance, strong and determined as always.

"Sacha?"

She made no reply, but found herself sniffing in response. She blinked the remnants of her tears away quickly and wiped her runny nose on the back of her hand. She did not want Alexei to see her as a snotty mess.

"I heard you had some trouble today, my pet," he said,

smoothing his hand over her hip as he walked around the bed and looked down at her miserable form. Sacha scowled at him then hid her face in the sheets. Her bottom was still throbbing and aching where the cane had bit dead across the center of her cheeks. The passing of time did not seem to make much difference to the discomfort. Somehow Vladimir had punished her in a way that just kept hurting.

"Talk to me, Sacha," he said with surprising softness in his voice. She chanced looking up at him to see that his gaze was far more sympathetic than she had imagined.

"You heard correctly," she said, trying to sound composed, though it was difficult when she knew she looked utterly pathetic. She covered her face with her hand, hiding the marks Svetlana had left.

"Vladimir caned you after finding you fighting?"

"That was not a fight," Sacha said quickly. "If I had been fighting, there would not be a mark on me, and your little bitch would be in pieces, I promise you that."

"There are marks on you? Let me see."

His gaze went toward her rear, where the cane lines were quite evident under the short dress she had been wearing.

"No," she scowled, covering her bottom even though it hurt to do so. The movement made the sheet slide from her face, where three bright red and surprisingly deep scratches still marked her cheek.

Alexei drew in air between his teeth. "She nearly hit your eye," he observed with displeasure. "Have those been cleaned?"

"No," she grumbled. "I was attacked, but the first thing anybody did was beat me for being the victim. Your majordomo is a major dick."

Alexei snorted as he reached down, wrapped his hand around her upper arm, and eased her up from the bed. "Let's go to the bathroom," he said. "Those scratches need cleaning."

Sacha didn't really have much in the way of choice as she was led to the bathroom, her unwilling feet making the journey behind Alexei's tall frame.

Once in the bathroom, he gently disrobed her. They saw the effects of Vladimir's punishment at the same time in the grand mirror. Her bottom was welted and bruised across the center of both cheeks. The skin around the visible cane marks, which themselves were blue, was red and angry.

"He certainly did not spare you," Alexei said. His voice seemed strained. Sacha did not know if that was because he was angry at her, or angry at Vladimir for caning her. Perhaps he was feeling some soft protective impulse toward her… ha! She laughed inwardly at the thought of that. There was nothing soft in Alexei.

"He hates me," she said. "Just like you do."

"I don't hate you, and nor does Vladimir for that matter," Alexei replied. "He was doing his job, which is to maintain order."

"Where I am concerned, but not where Svetlana is concerned. None of this was my fault." Sacha pouted miserably as Alexei gently dabbed disinfectant over the scratches on her face. It stung, but what was a little more sting when her rear was on perpetual fire? "She started it."

Alexei let out a gentle chuckle. "You sound like a whelp," he chided.

"She attacked me," Sacha continued. "And then Vladimir beat me and not her. It wasn't fair!"

"He caned you because you gave him attitude, and he let her off because she was appropriately contrite."

Obviously they had spoken on the subject. Sacha had no doubt that Vladimir probably exaggerated what she had said in order to justify his brutal discipline.

"You mean she lied to his face and said she was sorry even though she wasn't," Sacha said bitterly. "Is that what you want your pack to be? A pack of liars who tell you what you want to hear?"

"Mind your temper," Alexei warned. "You have been in enough trouble today already."

Sacha felt very sore and extremely sorry for herself. Life

in the Russian pack was not fair. Most of the time it was the precise opposite of fair, and Alexei seemed to care more about appearances than truths. As long as everyone made the right noises and looked the part, a blind eye was turned.

She pulled away from him and scowled. "Does the truth mean nothing to you?"

"You are confusing being truthful with being rude and disrespectful. A common mistake," he said patiently. "Come here and let me finish cleaning you. You do not want these scratches to go septic and scar your pretty face."

"If she so much as looks at me again, I will tear her throat out," Sacha vowed.

"You will do no such thing," Alexei growled at her, lowering his voice to a serious timbre. He pulled the cloth away and locked eyes with her in that way he had that somehow made his face take up the entire field of her vision. "You will avoid unnecessary conflict at all costs."

"I was attacked," she reminded him yet again. "I did avoid the conflict. She will come for me again unless I do what is necessary. Or are you so weak you allow bitches to cause unrest under your nose?"

"There is only one troublesome bitch under my nose at this point," Alexei replied grimly.

Again Sacha found herself cast in the role of troublemaker. It was not fair. Why would they not listen to her? Why was Alexei, who had been initially sympathetic, now turning on her too?

"The woman is infatuated with you," Sacha explained. "She thinks her rightful place is in your bed. She threatened me because I sleep in your bedchamber and because she could smell your scent on me."

"What Svetlana thinks is Svetlana's business," Alexei replied. "It is natural for girls to have dreams and designs on their alpha."

"So you like the fact that there are women whose panties get wet when you walk by," Sacha snapped at him. "A willing harem just begging for your cock."

"Don't be crude, pet," Alexei chided her gently. "I am simply saying that the fantasies of single females are not to be taken seriously. It is even more pronounced when they come into heat, as I suspect Svetlana must be. Once she is mated, she will forget her desires."

"And why does she not have a mate?"

"She has refused all those who would have her."

"Because she has her designs on a higher prize—you." Sacha snorted. "You are a fool, Alexei."

His hand landed hard against the outside of her left cheek, making her squeal in outrage and pain. "Mind your tongue, pet."

The punishment, though it was small, coming as it did on top of more unfair punishment left Sacha furious at Alexei. Every single person in the pack was impossibly cruel to her and she was tired of it.

"Don't speak to me that way," she said, her tone regaining some of its old imperious strength. "I am nobody's pet and I tire of this game you insist on playing with me. I am no pup to be chastised. I am almost as powerful as you are."

He let out a short laugh, as if her arrogance amused him. "Pet, you do not know what power is." He finished cleaning the scratches and nodded in satisfaction. "Shower and dress for dinner," he said. "I would have you at my side tonight."

Sacha's ears perked up at that and almost made her forget her temper. Being by his side meant showing Svetlana just how wrong she was. Sacha rather looked forward to seeing the expression on the woman's face when she realized that the alpha truly had made his choice—and it was not Svetlana.

He pressed a kiss to her forehead and ran his hand over her bottom soothingly. "Come and find me in my office when you are ready, pet."

• • • • • • •

Though she was not in the mood to obey, and though she was still rather angry at Alexei for taking Vladimir's side in the matter of the caning, she did obey his order to prepare for dinner.

Sacha showered, dried her hair, and put it up atop her head before selecting something from the wardrobe Alexei had provided for her. She chose a black lace gown that had been carefully designed to provide just enough modesty to be suitable as public attire, but that allowed the curve of her form to be appreciated by anyone who might cast a glance in her direction.

It was with no small measure of pride that she presented herself to Alexei some time later. His response was just as gratifying as she had imagined it would be.

His eyes widened, his pupils dilating as a slow, wolfish smile spread over his handsome face. "You look absolutely beautiful, pet."

Sacha allowed herself a smile as he rose and pressed a passionate kiss on her lips. Her body melted against his, aided by the liberal application of his palm as it first ran down over her back and hip, then swatted her bottom multiple times, imparting a sting over the lines of the cane, which served to stimulate her hips against his body and made the swelling erection in his pants grow hard along her belly.

His tongue pillaged her mouth and she felt his hunger as a primal thing just barely contained by body and will. When he broke the kiss, she felt a little dizzy and out of breath.

"I would feast on you all night long," Alexei growled down at her. "But the pack are waiting for us and we must make our appearance."

Our appearance. When he spoke like that she could almost fantasize that she was his mate, the female alpha. The queen of the pack. Sacha allowed that illusion to take hold as she was led to the dining hall, a grand space in which most of the pack were already assembled.

There had been a lively amount of chatter before their

entrance, but as Alexei and Sacha stepped into the room, a hush fell over the gathered pack. Sacha held her head high, feeling many dozens of eyes upon her, some approving, some lustful, some jealous, some simply interested. In that moment, she felt as much like her old self as she ever had. Alexei had put her front and center, sending a strong message to the pack at large. She was not some stray to be tolerated. She was a powerful female who had their alpha's ear… and a lot more besides.

Glancing over the hall, Sacha saw that the pack ate as one group across three tables. There was the head table at which Alexei and Vladimir and a couple of others sat, and two other long tables that ran perpendicular from its edges down the middle of the hall, creating a horseshoe shape.

The pack had come hungry and eager to eat, but there was an order to everything. As Alexei entered, the whole pack stood. It was clear then that nobody sat until Alexei sat. Nobody drank until he had his first sip of wine. Not a soul in the room made any movement without reference and deference to him. It was a thing of beauty to see the way every individual acted in accordance with the will of the group, not because they were forced to, but out of respect for the alpha and for their pack.

Sacha smirked as she caught Svetlana's jealous gaze. The single women were sitting at the far end of the tables, about as distant from the alpha as was possible, denoting their diminished rank. There were a few partnered women sitting further up the table, but they did not seem as concerned by Sacha as the singles did. Svetlana's glare was almost palpable even at that distance as she shot daggers at Sacha, willing only the worst of things upon her. Sacha made sure to make eye contact with Svetlana and smile a little more broadly than before. She might still bear the marks of Vladimir's cane on her rear, but there was no doubt that though Svetlana had won the battle, Sacha had won the war.

After greeting the pack, Alexei sat down. Sacha made to take the chair next to him, but he pushed it aside and pointed to the carpeted floor instead. She looked at him, confused.

"By my side," he said. "On your knees on the floor. I will feed you from my hands, to save you the humiliation of eating from a bowl."

A hot flash ran through Sacha's body. So this was not meant to elevate her, but to further embarrass her. Instead of sitting by his side as an equal, he was putting her on display to the pack as a whole, in front of the woman who had challenged her earlier that day, no less. She stared at him, shocked at his expectations of her. She would rather have had Vladimir apply another six strokes of his damned cane than take a position on the floor. No other pack member was deprived of the privilege of a chair; why should she be relegated to the carpet?

Seeing the rebellion in her gaze, Alexei ran his hand through her hair and gently took a fistful of it at the back of her head as he leaned in and murmured to her, "Better to obey and please me than be punished in front of the pack, no?"

"You are a bastard," she growled back at him in muted tones that only he could hear. He tugged at her hair and Sacha found herself at the mercy of his strength as he pushed her down to her knees next to his chair. Sitting on the floor, she could not be seen over the table; it was almost as if she was not there at all.

She found herself between Alexei and Vladimir, who for his part paid her no mind whatsoever. The meal began without anyone commenting on the way she had disappeared from view, and soon food was being delivered and consumed. The conversation picked up all around her, but left to her own devices on the floor, her fine gown pressed against the carpet, Sacha retreated into stony silence.

It was impossible to find a comfortable position. Her bottom was still sore from the caning Vladimir had given her, so sitting on it was out of the question. She ended up resting her weight along one thigh and the underside of her hip, propping herself up with one arm in what probably looked like a relaxed pose, but wasn't.

· · · · · · ·

Alexei smiled down at his good little pet. He knew it was taking every ounce of self-control Sacha had to stay in place and not rebel against his desires, but this was part of the training. Obedience first, then reward would follow.

He knew too, that she thought her treatment was unfair. He could see it in the set of her lips and the fire in her eyes. Sacha could say so much with her eyes, enchanting and dark. They drew him in and almost made him feel guilty for putting her through this training so soon after Vladimir's punishment. The silent question was almost audible. "Why? Why me? Why now?"

It would have felt kinder to her if he had let her stay in his room, have food sent to her, but that would have isolated her from the pack. Alternatively, he could have sat her with the other females; however, given the conflict there, it would have been more counterproductive than having her at his feet. She would have liked to sit beside him, but she had not earned that position and the pack knew it. Though Sacha thought him cruel, having her kneel by his side was as kind as he could afford to be.

Little did she know that far from being laughed at by the others, her position, even sitting at his feet, was a coveted one. Svetlana would have fallen over herself for the chance to snuggle by his side. Not that Sacha was snuggling. She was now sitting almost bolt upright, her spine straight, her expression stoic. She would have done anything to hide the shame she so clearly felt, but in spite of her stoicism it was coming off her in waves. Alexei wished she felt pride rather than shame, but he could not control her emotions, only her actions. So he sat and ate dinner with a sullen pet by his side who shook her head and tightened her lips every time he offered her a morsel. She would not eat a thing, even when he gave her a warning glance. He thought about threatening to take her over his knee there in the dining hall and spank her before the pack, but he could see that she was trying to behave in a manner of speaking, she just didn't know how to accept the position she found herself in. Instead of punishing her, he sat with her and let her sulk as long as she needed to.

• • • • • • •

After dinner the men lapsed into conversation. Alexei reached his hand out to Sacha and let his fingertips run lightly through her hair, his fingernails scratching her scalp. He expected her to stiffen and move away, but to his surprise she not only tolerated the caress but leaned into it. He glanced down to see her eyes half closed in a catlike expression of comfort.

She caught him looking at her and immediately pulled away. He felt a twinge of pity for her. She could not allow herself to enjoy him even a little because she was so intent on keeping her pride. Small moments of stolen pleasure had to be denied and disavowed as quickly as possible. If only she could allow herself to enjoy the fruits of submission rather than constantly denying herself every kind of nourishment.

"Come, pet," he said, reaching his hand down to hers. "It is time we retired for the evening."

He helped her up to her feet and admired the way she rose gracefully in spite of her embarrassment. Sacha had an almost regal presence at times, something he couldn't have taken from her no matter what he did. If only she knew that, she might not be so resistant.

She stood with her head held high as the eyes of the pack turned upon them and several dozen voices bade the alpha goodnight. He held her hand tightly, feeling her desire to be away from them as quickly as possible. She still didn't understand that even sitting on the floor, sharing space and time with the pack was how the bonds would be formed. Even though she had been out of sight, her scent had mingled with theirs. It would have been better if she had eaten and shared the consuming of flesh with them, but he was glad enough for what she had experienced. He found little glimmers of hope in the few seconds she had allowed his caress, and the fact that she had submitted to his command to sit at his feet. Alexei was feeling quite content and proud of his pet as he led her from the dining hall back to his chambers.

Sacha was silent as she walked with him. He sensed she was processing the experience, both consciously and on a deeper, more animal level, which was far more important. The lessons he needed to teach could not be imparted in words. They were lessons of the soul and the older, deeper mind that allowed every shifter to tap into animal form.

He felt her responding to him in the way her hand gripped his just as tightly as he gripped hers. She pressed quite close to him, not quite touching, but so close that light barely broke between them. She was uncertain, perhaps even scared of the things she had felt while at his feet. He leaned over and pressed a kiss to the top of her head as he led her into the bedroom and let her slide onto the bed. Sacha did so in a languid, graceful motion that managed to keep the worst of the cane lines from having pressure upon them.

"Are you hungry, pet?"

She hesitated and lowered her lashes before answering him in a small voice, "Yes."

"You should have eaten what was offered to you at dinner," he said. He intended on feeding her, but a gentle scolding was still in order. She could not be allowed to think that passive means of avoiding his orders would be tolerated.

"Would you eat from my fingers if I were to force you to sit beneath the table like a dog?" She turned the question on him.

"If you were my alpha, yes. But that is not how things are, Sacha. You must come to accept your life as it is now, or you will cause yourself a great deal of pain." He spoke in gentle, but firm tones, which seemed to reach her.

She gave him an almost plaintive look. In spite of everything, she did seem to understand the position he was in. She just couldn't come to terms with hers.

"I will not have you starve," he said. "Food will be brought in a moment. But Sacha, at dinner time your place will be where you sat today. And I expect you to eat your dinner. Do you understand?"

She let out a sigh and retreated into her British wit. "How can I possibly eat a full meal from your fingers, Alexei? Will you cup your hands like a bowl? What if they serve soup?"

He allowed a small smile to cross his lips. "I will have a bowl set aside for you, my pet. And perhaps, if you are fortunate, your very own spoon."

"Oh," she said, clasping her hands to her chest. "Cutlery! I did not think I should ever be afforded such a grand privilege."

"Careful, pet," he growled softly. "That cheek will earn you a spanking, and your bottom is already sore enough, wouldn't you say?"

• • • • • • •

Sacha opened her mouth to retort, but fortunately for her a plate was brought at that very moment. Her stomach growled with hunger as she smelled the succulent roast chicken once more. Alexei thanked the deliverer and took the plate in his hands. She watched the food more than the man as he carried it across the room toward her, her mouth watering at the prospect of finally eating. It had been a very long day and she was famished. Resisting the tidbits he had offered her during dinner had been harder than she'd thought it would be.

She watched with widening eyes as he did not give the plate to her, but instead took a piece of chicken between his thumb and forefinger and held it out to her. "Eat."

She blushed. So it was not going to be as simple as she had hoped. Of course not. Alexei was going to make her bend to his will yet again. Anger rose in her as her eyes narrowed and she opened her mouth to give him a piece of her mind...

"Sacha," he said in deep, soft tones, cutting her off before she could begin. "You are hungry. Put your pride aside for a moment and eat."

His eyes held hers and she saw more than mere dominance there. This was care. He wanted her to eat and he wanted the act to be intimate. He wasn't trying to shame her; he was trying to bond with her.

Sacha let her lips part, their eyes never leaving one another as Alexei slipped the chicken into her mouth. She savored the rich flavor of the meat, the spices that had seasoned it, and the delicious fat that had sunk into the meat while it was cooking.

How many times before had she eaten chicken just like this and never noticed all the sensations that accompanied the act of eating? She found herself suddenly aware of the way her whole body responded to the food, an anticipatory warmth in her stomach and a rush of well-being that flowed through every part of her.

Alexei smiled and picked up another piece of chicken. This he did not have to convince her to open her mouth for. Her lips parted, welcoming the nourishment. On an animal level, she knew that the food was his and she ate by his leave and yet in that moment she did not experience that fact as humiliating. Instead she could feel the care he was taking to demonstrate how he wanted to look after her.

All of these messages were imparted without words, through his actions and his demeanor. He smiled gently as she ate, seeming thoroughly pleased at both her compliance and her willingness to allow his care.

They had fucked on their first meeting and many times since, but this was almost more intimate than sex had been. Sacha found herself starting to moisten, little trickles of liquid excitement forming between an entirely different set of lips. Her hips started to squirm back and forth as she lapped at his fingers, suckling them with suggestive motions of her tongue.

Alexei caught the shift in her mood and put the plate to the side. One appetite had been sated, but another was growing between them.

He joined her on the bed, turning her onto her back as he covered her body with his own. She let out a little whimper of discomfort as her sore rear came into contact with the sheets, but Alexei paid little mind. He was too busy kissing her, sliding the straps of the dress from her shoulders and tugging it down her body to leave her in nothing but a small pair of underwear.

"No brassiere, pet? And here I was thinking you do not enjoy being displayed."

Sacha responded by taking either side of his shirt in her hands and pulling roughly, buttons popping off as his hard torso came into view. He chuckled and pulled his suit jacket off, helping her to disrobe him. Soon clothing scattered the floor and they were both naked, his hands cupping her breasts, his tongue rasping over her nipples as she arched off the bed and moaned, pressing the damp nexus of her thighs against the hard muscle of his leg.

His cock was fully erect, pre-cum dripping from the head, but he did not push it inside her waiting chalice. Instead he teased her. Every time her hips rose toward him, her flowering lower lips hoping to capture his rod, he would nip the side of her neck and growl a warning, or pinch a nipple just hard enough for her to retreat.

"Such a greedy little pet," he chided as he slid down her body and pressed his tongue to her slit. Her lower lips parted for him and she felt a rush of warmth and pleasure as he began to lap at her pussy, his warm, wet tongue running over the folds of her sex and circling the hard little nub of her clit. She had eaten and now it was his turn to consume.

His hot tongue brought her to gasping climax after gasping climax three separate times before her begging and pleading for his cock finally broke his resolve and he pushed himself deep inside her pussy.

Sacha let out a cry of pure pleasure as she was filled by him. She was certain that nobody on earth could love her as Alexei did. He surged inside her and it was not just her body that responded, her tight inner walls wrapped around him, her lips gripping his cock as he slid in and out... but her very soul seemed to be transported to a higher place when they were connected at the loins. Two spirits, one beast, that was how it felt as Alexei skillfully thrust toward an orgasm that left her quaking on his cock, her hips writhing as he held himself deep inside her and let her greedy pussy clench and massage his cock for all it had.

Still he was not done with her. As her fourth climax faded, he started to stroke in and out of her again. Sacha's pussy was starting to ache, and her bottom was still sore so there were a few whimpers mixed in with the moans, but her wetness never abated. She could see her juices gleaming on his shaft, testament to just how much she wanted him.

Alexei slid his hand between her thighs and for a moment she felt a tickling sensation between her cheeks. She gasped and her eyes went wide as he pulled his cock out of her for a moment and let his fingers swirl inside her, gathering her juices. He pushed his hardness back inside her and his fingers drifted lower. As he fucked her languidly, he let the tips of his wet fingers run lightly around her bottom hole, teasing that tight aperture.

It made Sacha blush to have him touch her there, but it also made her clit throb and her pussy ache for more and so it was with grace that she allowed him to play with her ass, tapping, teasing, circling, and finally pressing the tip of a finger into her tight little bottom at the same time as his much larger cock stretched her pussy.

"Every part of you belongs to me," he growled down at her possessively. She could feel him growing thicker inside her, a sure sign that his orgasm was not far off. He seemed to enjoy the way her tight ass was gripping his finger, the way she whimpered when he pushed it deeper. There was no doubting it, Alexei enjoyed his dominance, and she was utterly submissive to him in that moment, her body consumed in an erotic haze, mind fogged by multiple orgasms as he fingered and fucked her to a final climax that made him slam deep inside her, his cum streaming into her well fucked pussy as her ass clenched around his finger, enhancing the climax beyond sense and sensation until the whole world seemed to be one glorious realm of pleasure.

CHAPTER SIX

If only the peaks of orgasm could have defined her experience with the Russians, all would have been well for Sacha. As time went by and days turned into weeks it may have looked as though she was settled in her new home, but she still thought of it as the Russian pack and no matter how much she seemed to bond with Alexei, her dreams were always of Darkwood and the English moors upon which she had grown up. Night after night she would fall asleep in the alpha's arms and dream of England. During the day she would take refuge in her own thoughts, separated as she was from the rest of the pack by Svetlana's hostilities. Though weeks had gone by since the bitch had attacked her, and though no further mention of the incident had been made, Sacha knew the matter had not been put to rest.

One overcast afternoon she sat at the window of Alexei's office, gazing out across the snowy plains and the thick forest beyond. There was a whole world out there, but it did not feel like it, locked as they were in cold and ice. The isolation was what had kept the Russian pack safe and thriving, but it made her feel further from home than ever before.

"Why so morose, pet?" His fingers curled through her

hair.

"No particular reason." She told the lie and forced a smile.

"You are homesick." It wasn't a question; he said it as a statement of fact. And he was right. She was homesick. As the weeks had passed by and life had gotten easier to some extent, her yearning for home had not abated. As much as Alexei tried to make her comfortable in her role as his pet, she could not easily forget how it had been to run a pack, to look out at the world around her and feel as if it were hers to command. The moors had been her territory, but these snowy plains were not. She felt marooned, utterly alone in a way nobody in Voindom could possibly understand.

She made no reply to his words and his fingers curled in her dark locks and tugged lightly. "We will speak later, pet. I have business to attend to." He used his grip to tilt her head back and brushed his lips lightly across hers. "Do not be so sad. All is well."

He left her with the words that seemed hollow to her. All was not well. She was the plaything of an alpha who would not make her his mate, she was the pariah of the pack she lived with, and she was an exile from the land she came from. By any definition of 'all' and 'well' the statement did not apply.

Sacha left his office, not wanting to intrude on his work, or have his presence intrude on her misery. She went to the library, the quiet atmosphere of which was perfect for rumination. Unfortunately for her, it was also one of the places Svetlana seemed to frequent. After less than an hour, the two women crossed paths. Some might have said it was an accident, though if the absolute truth were to be known it was far more likely that an unconscious animal instinct to finish the business that had started there and settle the claim of territory drew them both to the same corner of the large room, away from the prying eyes of others.

"Englishwoman," Svetlana said, her eyes narrowed, her lips curled up in an unpleasant smile. "Still here, I see."

"Svetlana, still sniffing around Alexei's drawers," Sacha replied with barely restrained glee. "Can you smell him on me?"

"You reek of cum," Svetlana agreed, though this time the fact did not seem to incense her. "That means nothing. Alexei uses you like other men use old socks. Somewhere convenient to dump their seed until someone worthwhile comes along. If you meant a thing to him, you would be his mate. But you are not. You are just his toy. His pet."

The barb hit home. Sacha felt her anger rise as Svetlana spoke the truth she was so afraid of. When she was in Alexei's arms, there was no doubt that he cared for her. She could hear it in his voice, see it in his eyes, feel it in his touch. But the moment he left her to her own devices, doubts like the ones Svetlana gave bitter voice to rose in Sacha more powerfully than ever before.

"You don't belong here," Svetlana smirked, sensing that she had found something that caused pain. "The only reason you're here is because your pack exiled you. Nobody wants you."

"Alexei wants me." Sacha did not like how defensive she sounded.

Svetlana's smirk only grew wider. "He uses you like you should be used—like the little whore you are. We laugh at you, you know. When you sit beneath the table at dinner time and he feeds you from his fingers, we have never seen anyone look so ridiculous. You are his slave, Englishwoman. And your place is beneath us all."

Sacha was not sure how, perhaps it was simply feminine instinct, but Svetlana was managing to play her like a piano, hitting every sour note. Rage began to rise in Sacha and though she knew she would certainly be punished for what she was about to do, she no longer cared. The color had drained from her cheeks, her heartbeat was pulsing in her ears, and every instinct she had was telling her to tear Svetlana apart.

It was time Svetlana learned the real consequences of

challenging an alpha female—for that was what Sacha was and always had been. Alexei could make her sit on the floor all he liked. He could humiliate her in a thousand little ways, but it would not change the truth of who and what she was.

Part of her was almost grateful for the opportunity Svetlana had given her, a reason to throw off the shackles of expectation and obedience and simply unleash what she was deep inside. As she raged, the animal began to flow inside her and make itself known on the outside. Her teeth grew longer, her clothes ripped and fell away as a much more powerful furred body emerged. In seconds, the restrained Englishwoman was gone, replaced with a vicious beast with one victim in mind.

"No!" Svetlana panicked. "You're not allowed to shift, it is forbidden, it is... Aiiiieeee!" Her frightened words became a squeal as Sacha took her to the floor, her powerful wolf form devastatingly effective against Svetlana's delicate female form.

Seconds later, Sacha's teeth made contact with Svetlana's screaming neck. Sacha did not know why the woman had not shifted. Perhaps she did not know how. Maybe she was ashamed of her animal form. Or maybe she was just scared of tearing her pretty dress. Whatever the reason, Sacha could feel her prey's frightened pulse underneath her tongue. It was exciting, to sense living blood beneath her and to know that she held the power of life and death over her rival.

Svetlana knew it too. She trembled beneath Sacha, paralyzed with fear. The stench of it was thick around her, further arousing Sacha's animal instincts. It took everything Sacha had not to unleash her full fury upon Svetlana—but the little bitch did not deserve death. Instead of doing anything that would harm her permanently, Sacha toyed with Svetlana's flailing form, enjoying the way she squealed and begged for help.

On some level, Sacha was aware that others had been alerted. She could sense movement at the periphery of her senses, but she was far too focused on teaching Svetlana a lesson in manners… until a sharp sting in her rump caught her attention.

She lifted her head and turned to see a dart sticking out of her fur. Vladimir was standing a few feet away, holding a small gun in his hand. As her consciousness began to fade and her wolf form slid into human shape, she let out a little snort of derision. So this was how it was in Voindom; they brought tranquilizer darts to wolf fights. Pathetic.

• • • • • • •

Sometime later, Sacha woke up groggy and on a thin mattress in what looked to her like a cell. For a moment, she thought she was back in England, in Lorcan's bad books, but as memory returned she realized that history had repeated itself. She was incarcerated once more.

Rather than feeling scared or sad, Sacha laid on her back, hands behind her head and smirked at the ceiling. In many respects, this had been the inevitable result. She wondered where Alexei would have her exiled to next. Perhaps somewhere exotic, maybe warmer. Somewhere in Asia, perhaps.

The man himself came in not long after she came to consciousness, brimming with anger. She could feel it coming from him in waves and though it should have frightened her, and once would have, at that moment all it made her feel was more defiant than ever.

"I told you to stay out of trouble," he snapped. "I told you to leave Svetlana alone, and I especially told you that shifting is forbidden without my permission!" He stopped next to the bed and stared down at her with stormy eyes.

She smirked up at him. There was no longer any point in playing submissive. She was not submissive; taking her frustrations out on Svetlana had reminded her of that. Taking wolf form had made everything clear to her. Some wild things could be tamed and made pets—but she was not one of them.

"You could have killed her," Alexei snapped when she remained silent.

"Yes," Sacha agreed, her tone cocky. "I could have. And I did not. Remember that."

Alexei ignored her remorseless disobedience in favor of repeating himself. "I forbade you to take your wolf form…"

"Yes," Sacha said again. "You did. Have you forbidden everyone here that right? Svetlana did not know how to defend herself. You have mocked me for being small and weak, but I have not seen a single person here take their wolf form once."

"It is not safe to…"

"Safe!?" Sacha burst out laughing. "You speak of safety like a coward. We are wolves, Alexei. Well, some of us." She looked him up and down with undisguised derision. "You act as if you are the ultimate alpha. And yet you deny your pack the one thing that makes them what they are." She let out a little sort of disdain. "Even Lorcan is stronger than you."

With a growl of anger, Alexei reached the end of his tether. Sacha was all out of luck, and he was all out of mercy. The room cartwheeled as he grabbed and spun her, his palm meeting her ass with a sound like a gunshot. She was still naked from having shifted from wolf to woman, and that gave him easy access to spank her bottom, her thighs, and even her pussy. He did not spare an inch of her intimate area, thrashing her as long and as hard as his powerful arm would allow him to.

The pain peaked quickly, a searing heat and ache that consumed her nethers, but Sacha knew how to ride it now and instead of wailing for mercy she cried out with subversive pleasure, her back arching, her thighs parting as she displayed a pussy that was wet with arousal she could no longer deny.

Her scent filled the room, womanly need making Alexei growl as his cock hardened in response. Just as she had known he would, he pinned her face down on the mattress, parted her thighs, and moments later his cock was deep inside her, thick flesh parting her lips and pushing into her pussy in one long, hard, dominating stroke that showed no regard for her spanked, swollen lower lips.

Sacha felt a welling of triumph. Even the hardest fucking was pleasure when she was this wet. He might think he was teaching her a lesson, but he was giving her exactly what she wanted... right up until he slid his hard cock out of her pussy and pressed the juice-soaked head toward the smaller aperture of her ass.

She let out a series of whimpers as he began pushing his cock inside her, making her bottom spread for him. It was not an easy passage to assail, but persistence and the ample wetness of her pussy allowed him to slowly slide deep inside her inch by inch.

"You will obey me, Sacha..." The words were growled in Sacha's ear, her naked body arched due to the firm grip Alexei had in her hair, dark tresses gathered in his fist.

"No, I won't," she hissed through gritted teeth. "I am not your pet and you are not my alpha. I have no alpha."

He thrust himself harder inside her, his cock penetrating deep in her ass. It was her own traitorous body that made his conquest possible as he rubbed lubrication from her flowing pussy over his cock, pushing himself deep into her bottom with long, insistent strokes. Sacha was shocked at how it felt to be taken that way. She had always thought it would probably hurt, but instead she felt very full, very stretched... and very small. The difference between him sliding between her nether-lips and taking her bottom was stunning. This way her pussy was empty, her clit bereft of stimulation, and yet she was very definitely being fucked toward orgasm regardless.

She could feel Alexei's cock pulsing inside her as his growls and grunts became more guttural and animal. He was taking out his frustration on her tender little ass and he was not holding back. Sacha reached underneath herself and began rubbing her own clit, which made the denied pleasure suddenly burst forth, her pussy clenching on emptiness as her ass was filled over and over, his hips slapping her cheeks as he accelerated to a hard crescendo and let out a dominant cry, coming in her bottom, filling her tightest hole with his seed.

When he was done with her, he slid from her body and pulled her upright to face him. Sacha met his gaze with her chin held high, her eyes meeting his without shame even though she could feel his cum dripping from her ass and running down her thighs. She had been claimed roughly, punished with a hard fucking and still she clung to defiance. If anything, the orgasm that she had been denied made her all more fiery in her response. Her clit was sore and throbbing, her pussy was as wet as it had ever been, and yet she knew she would not be getting what her body so desperately desired.

"Do we have an understanding, Sacha? You do not shift without my permission, and you certainly will never put your teeth on another pack member."

It was the strangest thing, to be told by an alpha wolf that she could not behave as nature dictated she should behave. Sacha would not stand for it.

"You don't understand, do you," she blazed at him. "You don't understand that I will never, ever allow myself to be subordinate to a lesser female, or male for that fact. I cannot be controlled, Alexei. Not by Lorcan, not by you. Not by anyone. I am an alpha through and through. It is my blood and my destiny and all your little games and collars can't change that."

Her announcement did not please him, as she knew it would not. "You were cast out of your pack," he said, his eyes burning cold fire into hers. He had a gaze like a blizzard, sharp and freezing her to her very core. "Exiled. You have no place. No home. No pack. So you can forget about throwing your weight around in my territory. You are not alpha. You are not even omega. You are my pet."

He was saying the same thing Svetlana had said, in a slightly different way, perhaps, but his words confirmed what she had felt from the outset. She was not welcome and she would never be a part of this pack. At least Svetlana had been honest about her feelings from the beginning. Alexei had pretended to welcome her and had made use of her body while harboring the same feelings toward her as the bitch did. Well, she would not wait to become an exile again.

"You are no alpha," she threw the words back at him. "You are too afraid even to take your natural form. You are a domesticated, neutered little pet, and I am done with you and your pack."

A moment later, the change came over her without thought. Alexei had forbidden it, but the animal part of her did not care what he had said. Her reaction was more about fear and rage and pure instinct than disobedience—that was merely a bonus. As she flowed into wolf form, she felt fresh freedom rush through her veins. She was not part of this pack. She owed them no allegiance, and in her animal body she knew that. The human mind clouded things with hope and desire and higher emotions that only served to make her a slave to a man who forced her to endure indignity after indignity.

The first time she had shifted in Alexei's presence she had been overwhelmed by him. This time she was not. This time she turned tail and fled before she could be stopped by his command. She ran toward the closed door and did not stop but instead gathered speed and leaped at it. The door shattered at two hinges and burst out of the latch with a loud crashing sound as the splintered wood panels fell into the hall, setting Sacha free.

She ran for all she was worth, paying little attention to the people she passed or the ornaments that went flying in her wake. She slammed against a table upon which a large vase sat and was only barely caught by someone standing nearby. Finding the staircase, she skittered down it, her paws sliding over polished wood with a momentum that turned her into a furry missile as she headed for the main doors. They too, were closed, but a figure nearby did her the service of opening the door, which ultimately saved the ornate glass panes she would otherwise have to have leaped through.

Sacha ran down the stone stairs and kept going, not looking over her shoulder to see if she was being followed. She headed out into the snow, running past the statues that marked the driveway and out into the wilds. There was power in the motion, in taking herself away from those who had tormented her. Vladimir, Svetlana, Alexei, they were nothing more than vague constructs locked somewhere in her human mind far away from the beast logic that sent her toward the forest on the horizon.

A human would not have been able to tolerate the temperatures for very long, but her wolf body was designed for conditions like these. The cool of the air and the snow made it easier for her to run longer and harder than she otherwise would have been able to, and when she got thirsty the snow was a quick source of water to quench her thirst. She did not need to eat as yet; she would not absolutely need food for several days. For now, all she needed was the land and the snow and the cover of the trees that enveloped her.

CHAPTER SEVEN

Sacha kept moving until there were no sounds at all, until her body tired of the motion and then completely gave out, dumping her in the snow. The anger that had propelled her so far, so fast had also faded, and along with it the rampant triumph that had accompanied her rebellion. In its place was a hollow sensation growing in her belly. A wolf could survive on her own, but it was harder to be happy. She curled up on herself as snowflakes drifted down from a dark sky, coating her fur in a thin crust of ice, and dreamed of the fire at Darkwood Manor and the bed at Voindom. Either would have done in that moment.

The strangest thing about life was the way things could seem to be so clear one moment when experienced in anger, and yet completely opposite the next. She had been so certain that Alexei hated her and that she had no place in his pack. But why then, did she now crave him? Why was she dreaming of being curled up in his arms rather than blanketed by snow?

Alexei's face swam before her animal imagination. Now that the anger had faded, she knew she had made a mistake. A mistake it was too late to take back. Alexei was not just an alpha. He was the only alpha who had ever been capable of dominating her and making her feel safe—and she had attacked him and run away. He would no doubt be very glad to see the back of her.

She had failed twice in the pursuit of pack and family and now she was completely and utterly alone. She deserved it.

· · · · · · ·

It was night when the pack came. The moon was high as shadows started to slip through the trees. Sacha was fast asleep, curled up tight against the cold and dreaming animal dreams that were much more peaceful than those she suffered as a human.

They moved silently through the snow and would have come upon her while she was still sleeping had the wind not shifted and a sudden gust brought the scent of a dozen wolves flooding into her nostrils. Sacha woke in an instant, lifting her head to scan the surrounding areas. She had only seconds to flee, and she took them, all four paws taking traction against the snow as she launched herself into the darkness.

This time there was no escape. Many more paws thundered in her wake and she had not traveled more than a few hundred feet before a heavy body landed on hers. A large male had leaped from behind and now pushed her to the ground with his weight. Teeth closed around the fur at the back of her neck as she was pinned in place by a much larger, heavier, more powerful animal. Alexei.

He held her there until she whined submission and then he stood before her, his nose lowered to hers. His fur was tipped blond and his eyes were blue even as a wolf. He had an eerie presence that sent chills through her very soul. She stayed flat on her belly, protecting her internal organs just in case he had some ill intention. She did not sense it, but her fear demanded it. Many more wolves circled her, cutting off all avenues of escape. Her ears were pinned back against her head, her lips lifted to reveal canines as she snarled at some of them.

Alexei snapped in her direction and she cowered, whimpering with fear. Her body was an apology in motion, but he did not seem inclined to accept it; no matter how she prostrated herself and showed submission he simply kept prowling around her, keeping her pinned in position. She did not know why at first, but it soon became clear.

She heard voices as the members of the pack who had not shifted caught up with the main pack, bringing with them chains. A thick steel collar was put around her neck and to that a heavy chain was attached. It seemed to her to be a foolish thing to do, for it was obvious that she could shift out of it in a heartbeat. It was only effective at restraining her in her wolf form.

She tried to prove that fact, but as she tried to shift back she found herself unable. The process that was so natural she did not need to think about it so much as breathe into it, had been blocked in some fashion. The collar. It had to be the collar.

Alexei flowed to human form, standing in the snow naked and proud. He looked down at her with those stormy eyes, his face hard, stern, and even frightening in the moonlight.

"That's right," he said. "You didn't know it was possible to be kept in wolf form, did you? You want to be a beast so much? Very well. You will be treated as one."

Sacha whined and pawed at the collar, but it was not going anywhere. She was trapped in it, trapped in her wolf form, which had many advantages in terms of avoiding an embarrassing human punishment, but did not allow her to argue.

A vehicle drove up out of the darkness, the same van she had been tossed into on her first day with the Russians. Under Alexei's hard eyes, she was loaded back into it by men she did not know and chained to one of the seats.

A plaintive whine escaped her. She knew that she had

been wrong in everything she had said and everything she had done. Wrong to defy him. Wrong to disobey him. Wrong to run away. Wrong. Wrong. Wrong.

She wanted nothing more than to lick his face and apologize, but it was too late. Alexei was furious with her, and that fury would not allow for anything but punishment.

After a bumpy ride back to Voindom, Sacha was led to kennels like a dog and put away behind a chain-link fence. She spent the night curled up on a piece of sacking that smelled like turnips. It was a punishment worse than being caned or thrashed or humiliated by any terse lecture. She regretted having run, and now being held so close to the rest of the pack and yet kept away from them she felt more alone than ever.

Night turned into day and food was brought to her, slipped through a slot and dropped onto the ground. The meat would normally have interested her in her wolf form, but she could not muster hunger. She turned away from it and curled up on herself, whimpering softly whenever she heard footsteps in the distance.

Alexei must be furious with her. He did not come to see her, nor did he allow her any reprieve from her punishment. She did not know how long he would keep her there. Sometimes it seemed as though her world would forever be marked by bars. Sometimes she thought that was all she would ever deserve.

CHAPTER EIGHT

"You are angry at her," Vladimir noted as Alexei paced the floor of his office.

"Of course I am angry at her. She ran away."

"And we tracked her down and brought her back." Vladimir's dark eyes gleamed. "It felt good, did it not? To take our wolf bodies and engage in a true hunt. Little Sacha gave us that gift."

Alexei frowned at his beta. Vladimir was enjoying all of this far too much for his liking. Privately, yes, he could perhaps admit to himself that he had not felt as alive in many years as he did that night, tracking his wayward pet across the snow, chasing her down and reclaiming her. There had been a primal thrill to it that had escaped his experience for far too long... but seeing it as a gift? That was too much.

"She was disobedient, willfully. She disrespected me. She disrespected our pack, our home. If you had heard the things she said before she ran... Vladimir, she has no respect for me."

"No respect for you? I have watched that woman choke down her pride night after night to sit at your feet. Perhaps it is not that she does not have respect for you. Perhaps it is you who do not have respect for her…"

Alexei's eyes narrowed at his beta. "Thin ice, Vladimir," he warned in a growl.

Vladimir did not seem in the least bit concerned by the threat. "Running away is a natural response to feeling as though one is not part of a pack. Whelps run away all the time. We do not put them in the kennels for it. We whip their rears and we set them back among the pack. Why are you punishing her this way?"

"Because she could have killed herself."

"Because you love her," Vladimir said knowingly. "Your anger is out of proportion, Alexei. It is as it was with Katya. You were always harder on her than anyone else."

"I was not hard enough with her," Alexei said, his voice low and guttural. "Katya's death was preventable. If I had been sterner…"

"Her death was an accident. It was not your fault, Alexei. You must forgive yourself for it. If you keep punishing yourself—and Sacha—you will never have love again. This one is not like Katya. She will resent you for what you are doing to her. She is too proud."

Alexei turned to Vladimir, his lips twisting dryly. "You are advocating for her?"

"I have watched her transform from a frightened little bitch to a female who the others admire," Vladimir said. "There is talk among the women of sneaking out after dark and shifting. They are following their true nature, and they are doing it because she did it."

"Just like Katya before her," Alexei growled. "Why am I cursed with these women?"

"Cursed?" Vladimir uttered a short, humorless laugh. "You have had your pick of docile women for a long time, and you have not been interested. We both knew from the start that this one was different. You have been enchanted with her from the moment you met. I agreed that she needed discipline and training at first, but Alexei, you cannot lock her up in the kennels forever. And you cannot stop her from becoming what she is—especially where the females are concerned."

"So you are saying, forgive her lest she incite a rebellion from inside a locked kennel?" Alexei laughed. "Even she is not that powerful."

"I am saying forgive yourself and stop hiding from her."

"I am not hiding, Vladimir." Alexei's tone was sharp.

Vladimir took a deep breath, and a note of earnest care came into his voice. "The mourning period has gone on long enough, Alexei. It is time to let the pack be a pack once more. It is time you took a mate. And it is time that wolves once more patrolled these lands. The pack respects you too much to be disobedient en masse, but there is a restlessness in this house that will never be gone until we restore the old traditions and come together beneath the full moon as we did before Katya died."

"You are saying I should make Sacha my mate."

"I am saying she is already your mate," Vladimir replied boldly. "She has been from the moment you laid eyes on her. There has been far too much denial in this house over the years, Alexei. It is like a poison."

"You were the one who told me that she needed discipline," Alexei reminded him.

"And she does, of that there is no doubt, but the women cannot be suffered to make their own order as they do now. Blood has been shed already, and more will be shed if you do not take a mate."

"I have told Sacha not to engage with the others. And the others know well enough not to cause trouble."

Vladimir's brows rose as he took a deep breath. "They know no such thing. Women are always trouble. You know that well enough. Keeping Sacha separate is no long-term solution. Svetlana has her instincts too, and they do not listen to any law but animal law."

"Tell me then, Vladimir, what is it you think I should do? If I accord Sacha status, I will undo every message we have given her since her arrival. It will encourage the very behavior that saw her exiled in the first place. And if I do not, the others will continue to pick on her and she will continue to retaliate."

"That is a question only you can answer. But leaving her in the kennels will not solve your problem. The girls find it very amusing. Svetlana, in particular, credits herself with Sacha's attempted escape and subsequent humiliation."

"Then perhaps you should deal with Svetlana," Alexei said in suggestive tones.

"And you should deal with Sacha."

Alexei gave Vladimir a long, hard look, then laughed. "We have both allowed ourselves to be distracted, haven't we, Vladimir? Me with my fear of history repeating itself. You with your soft spot for a certain young lady..."

Something like color rose in Vladimir's cheeks and Alexei chuckled. Svetlana was still single not only because she refused all mates and because she had designs on the position of alpha bitch—but because Vladimir had a particular fondness for her that he never acted upon. It was time that changed.

CHAPTER NINE

After what seemed to her to be an endless incarceration, Sacha was thrilled to be taken from her kennel and walked through the mansion at the end of a heavy chain. What had once been humiliating was now a welcome alternative to the torment of being locked up alone. Three days had passed since her capture and she had not so much as caught scent of Alexei in that time. She missed him with all her mind and all her body. She physically ached to be near him and yet all she had was the concrete and the bars. The misery of confinement had weighed heavily on her animal spirit and she yearned to be human again.

As she was led to the alpha's quarters catching Alexei's scent made her whine with excitement. She strained at the end of the chain until another man joined in holding it and even then she dragged the two able bodies toward Alexei's office.

"Release her," Alexei said as she came through the doorway. "And leave us. Take the chain, leave the collar."

The men did as they were ordered. Sacha went forward and nosed his hand, inhaling his scent deeply. She had felt a horrible hole in her heart during their separation, a deep loneliness that she knew would only be assuaged when he forgave her.

Wordlessly, Alexei reached down and removed the collar. She sprawled from wolf to naked, sobbing woman in a matter of seconds. He swept her up into his arms and held her close as she cried with relief and guilt.

"I'm sorry," he said as she cried. "I should not have left you alone for so long. I needed to think."

"I'm sorry I ran away," she sniffed. "I'm sorry I made you so angry you hated me."

"I never hated you," he reassured her, pressing kisses to her tear-stained cheeks. "I love you, Sacha. And I owe you an explanation, as well as an apology."

She looked up into his face and saw that he was racked with as much pain as she was. Something was different between them, some barrier had been broken down and when she looked into his eyes, she saw more of the man than she had ever seen before.

"You owe me an apology?"

"Your life here has been miserable," he said, stroking her hair as he cradled her in his lap. "I know why you've been homesick. Not because you're so far from the place you grew up, but because you have not found a home here, with me. And that is my fault, Sacha. Your instincts have been correct from the beginning. Even your desire to dominate Svetlana. You cannot help that any more than you can help wanting to shift and to roam and to challenge me… and lose."

It was the first time he truly seemed to understand her. Sacha could only sit and listen, somewhat stunned by what she was hearing. For once he was not dictating orders to her; he was actually speaking with an open heart.

"I told you when you arrived here that you would be my pet," he said. "We made love within an hour of our first meeting and I knew then that you were much more than an amusement, but still I kept you from the place you were born to take. At first I did it for the sake of teaching you a much-needed lesson, but even when you learned it, I did not acknowledge that."

Sacha nodded her agreement. "I cannot be some quiet little pretty sweet thing, Alexei. And I will not allow other women to taunt me. If you whip me a thousand times, that will not change. And I will not abstain from my wolf form either. Even Lorcan did not deny his pack that, though he denied us everything else…" Her voice trailed off as Alexei pressed a gentle finger to her lips, silencing her for a moment.

"I was married once," he said, in what seemed like a digression, though Sacha had the sense to close her mouth and listen to what he was trying to tell her. "Her name was Katya and she loved the wild. She would take wolf form and she would travel for days, sometimes up to a week at a time. I allowed it because it made her happy to know the world in that way. She always returned to me and for a time she would be content and calm and then she would feel the call and be gone again. Then… one time, she did not return. We sent a search party on the seventh day." His voice became tight as his eyes grew wet. "And we found her on the ninth. There were two bodies—hers and the bear that had killed her."

"And that was when you forbade shifting," Sacha guessed.

"Yes," Alexei admitted. "The pack mourned with me. We turned one last time and since then, no more. It had been that way so long I think we had collectively forgotten what we once were. It was not until you ran the other night and we tracked you that we moved as a pack…" He gave her a solemn look. "Vladimir said I should thank you for that. Perhaps I should."

"Well," Sacha said. "You're welcome." She gave him a little, slightly sad smile, knowing that the subject was painful to him.

"After Katya, I thought there would never be another. As the years went by, I became convinced of it. But when you walked through the doors of our home, everything changed. I was just too consumed with old grief to admit it to myself. I knew I could not bear the loss of another mate, so I made you my pet. I put you in a position I could control. But I cannot control you, Sacha. No more than I could control Katya. The most beautiful spirits are those that remain untamed. I knew that once, but I let her loss take that knowledge from me. I let it take more than a decade of life from this pack. But I will not let it take any more joy, or cause any more pain."

"So, I am forgiven? And I am no longer your pet?"

He smiled at her hopeful expression. "There will still be consequences for your behavior, Sacha. But before I deal with you, there is someone else for us to deal with... Svetlana."

"Us?" Sacha's eyes brightened.

"You will stay quiet," he cautioned her. "I will allow you to see what is about to happen because I think it is important that this matter is settled once and for all. I will not tolerate any further conflict between the two of you, understand?"

She nodded solemnly, though on the inside she was burning with anticipation. What would Svetlana's punishment be? She almost didn't care; she was far too excited by the prospect of bearing witness to it.

• • • • • • •

Svetlana was summoned and arrived in quick order, likely excited by the prospect of a meeting with the alpha. As she came through the door to Alexei's office she looked pleased, but the smile fell off her pretty face when she saw Sacha sitting there next to Alexei, dressed casually in a dark robe that he had insisted she put on even though Sacha would have been quite happy to receive Svetlana naked. It would have sent a message that clothing could never convey. Vladimir was also present, though Sacha was not sure why. She hoped it was because she was about to see

Vladimir cane Svetlana's hide.

"Svetlana," Alexei said in stern tones that made Sacha quiver even though she was not the one in trouble. "From the moment Sacha arrived here, you have engaged in a campaign to make her life difficult. You have turned down mate after mate and remained a single agitator. That will not be allowed to go on another day. I have decided your mate for you."

"Oh?" Svetlana's lower lip trembled uncertainly.

"Vladimir will be your mate," Alexei declared.

"Vladimir? But he is…" she struggled for words, but found only one, "…old."

Vladimir snorted, but otherwise remained silent. Sacha watched the silent interaction between Svetlana and Vladimir with interest. They would make a fine couple. They shared a particular refinement and polish. In fact, now she looked at them more closely, they could have modeled for wedding cake toppers, they looked so perfectly matched.

"He is a few years younger than I," Alexei replied. "And he is uniquely equipped to deal with a mate who uses sly means to try to destabilize the pack."

Svetlana's face crumpled into despair and for a quick moment, Sacha almost felt sorry for her. Svetlana had been following her instincts and desires. It was not her fault her needs had been ignored for so long and allowed to become poisonous.

"Yes, sir," Svetlana said, completely deflated. Sacha noted that Svetlana didn't seem brave enough to actually look at Vladimir, which Sacha could understand. Vladimir was a different kind of dominant to Alexei, but he was undoubtedly dominant and she had no doubt that Svetlana would soon learn to behave under his watchful eye. He was maintaining his usual reserved silence in the moment, but Sacha was sure there would be little in the way of silence once he got his hands on his new mate, who even now was squirming and blushing at the thought.

"Alexei," Sacha said, speaking up though she had been

asked to be quiet. "May I speak to Svetlana alone for a few minutes?"

When Alexei, Vladimir, and even Svetlana looked dubious about the prospect, she added, "I have no intention of being in any way aggressive, I promise. I simply think we should talk. Much has passed between us."

"Very well, pet," Alexei agreed. "A few minutes, and we will be on the other side of the door. If there is any conflict at all, even so much as a raised voice, both of you will be thrashed. Understand?"

Sacha waited until the men had left the room before approaching Svetlana who stood with her head bowed, looking absolutely crushed. Sacha understood. Svetlana must have known she would never be Alexei's mate, but hearing it so directly and being given to another, that had to hurt.

"You must hate me," Svetlana mumbled. "Gloat all you like! I suppose you have earned it."

"You and I are cut from the same cloth," Sacha replied. "I do not blame you for what you did. I would have done the same. I have, in fact, done much worse."

Svetlana's expression was one of intense surprise. "You have?"

Sacha nodded. "Oh, much, much worse," she shared. "I put my brother's mate through hell and back. Almost killed her on two separate occasions, perhaps three."

Svetlana's fine brow raised at her, then she let out a laugh. "I believe that," she said, before the smile fell from her face. "Vladimir is to be my mate."

"Do you not like him?"

"It is not that I do not like him. He is handsome and he is strong," Svetlana said. "But he uses that cane so severely…"

"Which is precisely what you need," Sacha interjected with a smile.

Svetlana blushed, and covered her mouth with her hands. Sacha suspected there was a smile under her fingers.

Svetlana had never just wanted Alexei. She had wanted a powerful mate, and she had earned herself one.

"This may surprise you, but I would like for us to be friends," Sacha said. "Our score is settled."

"A friendship? After all that has passed between us?"

"We have spilled one another's blood," Sacha said. "There can be nothing more bonding, surely?"

A little laugh escaped Svetlana. "I think you are mad," she said. "But… perhaps."

"Perhaps is a good starting point," Sacha smiled, just as the door opened and Alexei and Vladimir came back into the room, both looking thoroughly suspicious.

"It was too quiet," Alexei explained. "We thought one of you might have snapped the other's neck."

Both Sacha and Svetlana allowed themselves quiet smiles as the men came forward and one by one, drew their respective mates away.

Sacha and Alexei ended up in their favorite place, the bedroom. Alexei pulled her down onto the bed and held her close, smiling down into her eyes.

"Satisfied, pet?"

"Very," Sacha said with a broad smile.

"Now, for your punishment," he said, slipping his fingers under her chin to keep her gaze on him. She looked up at him with no small measure of concern at the mention of punishment. Surely she had been punished enough?

"Your punishment," he said in gruff, intimate tones, "will be to be my wife, my mate, my lover, my pet for as long as I draw breath."

It felt to Sacha as though the breath had gone out of her. She felt her extremities begin to tremble as she tried to take in what he had said. His mate. That one little word meant everything to her. He was not just according her status, he was telling her that they were inherently equal. Though he had the greater authority, she was his counterpart. No longer would she be mistaken for some silly plaything or slave. She would be first among females, a leader among the pack.

"It is a harsh punishment that will last a lifetime," he said, his lips curling into a smile. "But I think you deserve it."

"It may very well be a mutual punishment," Sacha replied. "I do not promise to make life easy for you."

"Promise me one thing and one thing only," he said before his lips descended on hers in a passionate kiss, which he only broke to finish the remainder of his sentence. "That you will never run from me again."

"That, I promise," Sacha agreed, melting into his arms with pure joy and love in her heart. Since coming of age she had yearned for a mate powerful enough to take her in hand, intelligent enough to keep her there, and gentle enough to soothe her pain after even the most deserved punishments. Alexei was all of that and more—and he was not quite done with her yet.

"You are my mate," he said, moving to a sitting position. "But I love you as my pet too, so come here, my naughty little one. I have yet to give you a full reckoning for the way you spoke to me before you ran away."

Sacha blushed as she slid over his lap, her bottom raised high as he caressed her cheeks and began to spank her lightly, his palm meeting her cheeks with tender, loving slaps that caused little in the way of pain but ignited her arousal as they always had.

"My lover, my mate, my pet," he intoned as he swatted her bottom. "I will have you in my bed, at my side, and over my lap as long as we both shall live."

"Not precisely traditional vows, but they will suffice," Sacha quipped, squealing with laughter as Alexei swatted her a little harder. The laugh turned into a moan as his fingers slid down from her bottom between her thighs and cupped her pussy possessively, rubbing her clit and her lips for a moment or two before returning to the task of spanking her impudent bottom. Sacha sighed with pleasure and stretched out, spreading her legs for his pleasure and hers as she embraced her new life with a whole heart.

Finally, the exiled Englishwoman was home.

EPILOGUE

Three years later…

In a remote manor on the English moors, a television was broadcasting the end of the news segment.

"Today's good news story comes to us from Russia," the anchor declared.

"Russia, Johnny?" His pretty blond co-anchor spoke with a mixture of glee and excitement, as if Russia were the best word she'd heard that day.

"Russia, Pam." Johnny flashed gleaming white teeth as he read from the teleprompter. "Conservationists are taking credit after drone footage shows rare wolves thriving in Siberia. A pack unseen for the better part of a decade takes to the tundra on a sunny afternoon. Let's take a look!"

The feed cut to a picture showing a pack of wolves in the wild. For the most part they were either resting or patrolling here and there, alert noses, eyes, and ears lifted for signs of trouble. The reason for their behavior became clear as the camera zoomed in to catch sight of a very large male wolf and his smaller mate lying together in the sunshine, three pups playing over their backs and through their fur, nipping at paws and tails and one another in a display of rambunctious glee. Mother and father nuzzled affectionately as their offspring played their little games of war, while around them the pack kept watch over the alpha couple and their progeny.

After twenty seconds the camera returned to the studio, where Pam the anchorwoman was beaming from ear to ear.

"So sweet," she squealed at a level just below that which would make the mic overload.

"Adorable," Johnny agreed. "Now, to Jim with the weather. Jim, how's it shaping up for the weekend?"

Lorcan Wallace, the English alpha, hit the mute button on his television remote, turned to his young wife and smiled. "You have their presents picked out, right? Nothing too big; Sacha says we spoil them."

"That's the whole point of nieces and nephews," Hannah replied with a grin, snuggling into her husband. She was much smaller than him; most people were. Lorcan had a bulk and a demeanor that was dominant through and through.

"Hannah…" His tone turned into a playful growl as she pressed a kiss to his neck.

"Oh, shush," she said. "You can't stop me."

Lorcan's thick brow rose at the dark-haired little minx. "Oh, is that right?"

"Mhm!" Her green eyes gleamed with mischief as she lifted a finger and poked Lorcan's chest. "You. Can't. Do. Anything."

A second later, she squealed with glee as her husband hauled her over his lap and swatted her bottom not nearly hard enough to hurt.

From bitter beginnings and dark days, two packs had found new hope. As he spanked his very deserving brat of a wife, Lorcan could not help but smile. Sending Sacha away had been the hardest decision of his life, but her exile had turned her from a bitter, dangerous little bitch into a loving and very well loved mother and leader. Alexei had given her what she had needed for so very long, and he was more grateful to the Russian alpha than he could ever express.

"Have you learned your lesson yet?" He looked down at Hannah's squirming bottom and made the inquiry in mild tones.

"Never!" Hannah giggled.

"I didn't think so," he said, his handsome grin broadening as he turned fully to the task he most loved: handling his mischievous mate.

THE END

STORMY NIGHT PUBLICATIONS WOULD LIKE TO THANK YOU FOR YOUR INTEREST IN OUR BOOKS.

If you liked this book (or even if you didn't), we would really appreciate you leaving a review on the site where you purchased it. Reviews provide useful feedback for us and for our authors, and this feedback (both positive comments and constructive criticism) allows us to work even harder to make sure we provide the content our customers want to read.

If you would like to check out more books from Stormy Night Publications, if you want to learn more about our company, or if you would like to join our mailing list, please visit our website at:

www.stormynightpublications.com

17247981R00061

Printed in Great Britain
by Amazon